7

FATAL ACCIDENT

Henry Simmons was driving home after a quiet drink in a public house. The night was dark and wet, even dangerous, but the roads were familiar. From his car radio, soft music filled his ears; at home a loving wife was waiting for him and for her he had some good news. Then tragedy. Henry ran down a cyclist and Henry had been drinking. The police arrested him and suddenly his life became one of violence and terror. The cyclist died and could not be identified, then the thugs moved in. They threatened Henry and his family, and they attacked anyone who came to his aid. Then a keen young policeman was murdered. And all because Henry Simmons had been involved in a fatal accident.

Books by Peter N. Walker
in the Linford Mystery Library:

CARNABY AND THE HIJACKERS
CARNABY AND THE GAOLBREAKERS
CARNABY AND THE ASSASSINS
FATAL ACCIDENT

PETER N. WALKER

FATAL ACCIDENT

Complete and Unabridged

LINFORD
Leicester

First Linford Edition
published January 1990

Copyright © 1970 by Peter N. Walker
All rights reserved

British Library CIP Data

Walker, Peter N. (Peter Norman), *1936–*
Fatal accident.—Large print ed.—
Linford mystery library
I. Title
823′.914[F]

ISBN 0-7089-6840-6

Published by
F. A. Thorpe (Publishing) Ltd.
Anstey, Leicestershire

Set by Rowland Phototypesetting Ltd.
Bury St. Edmunds, Suffolk
Printed and bound in Great Britain by
T. J. Press (Padstow) Ltd., Padstow, Cornwall

1

THE car was going well.

It rode through the night cloaking its driver in an aura of cosy warmth, splashing its way through the patches of water which decorated the greyness of the road ahead. Occasionally, the lights would reflect from a pool of dark water and cast beams into the sky above, and now and then, an oncoming vehicle would momentarily dazzle the driver so that he slowed down to await the other's safe passage on his offside.

And all the time the rain poured down; it hissed against the red painted bodywork of the travelling Hillman and was picked off by the wind to be carried from the protruding parts of the vehicle when it was lost forever in the night. The splashing beneath him; the constant and rhythmic movement of the windscreen wipers; the hum of the soft music from the radio lulled the driver into a deep sense of well-being, cosiness and safety from the winter storm outside.

His car ate up the miles, carrying him nearer home at every turn of its wheels and he knew that Margaret would be waiting to hear his news. He could see her now, sitting before the television and glancing at the clock on the mantelshelf in a vain effort to estimate how much longer he would be; she'd have her favourite woollen sweater loose about her, her knees curled up on the cushions and the daily papers scattered around because the children were in bed, and couldn't therefore move them or draw on them. The fire would be getting low—it was late now. Nearly eleven fifteen, in fact, and almost time for bed. When he was safely home, Margaret would rustle up a cup of Horlicks for him, warm and sweet.

Only another eight miles to go. Twenty minutes at the outside. Here in the north, the roads were comparatively free from traffic and his journey from the pub would be trouble-free so far as hindering traffic was concerned. Not that he often went out to the pub.

In fact it was a rare occasion for him. Sometimes he popped across to the White Swan, nearly opposite his cottage in Drydale. There he'd enjoy a quiet drink, sometimes alone, sometimes with Margaret and sometimes with colleagues or friends. It obviated the need to drive after a drink; it eliminated the risk of a breathalyser check and it meant a gloriously short journey home afterwards.

Not like tonight.

Mr. Barnett, the District Manager, had telephoned this morning and said, "Henry. Got some good news for you. Can you be at the Three Tuns, Embleton, tonight—eight o'clockish?"

"Yes. Why? What's happened?" Henry had asked.

But Barnett had said, "Tell you tonight, old boy. Eight o'clock then?"

And so Henry had spent the day wondering what it was all about; Margaret had made a few inspired but unacceptable guesses.

"Promotion!" she'd said, wide eyed and enthusiastic. "Barnett's retiring. You've been appointed in his place."

"No," Henry had said. "District Managers like him don't retire so early. It won't be that."

"An extension of your area?" Margaret had been thinking of an increase in Henry's future earnings.

"I'd have known something about that in advance," had been his reply. "Unless somebody's got the sack on an adjoining area."

"You'd have known that, too."

"Yep. I would. I've done nothing wrong . . . besides, he sounded delighted over the phone. Not a critical sort of Barnett—just the opposite in fact."

"Won something? Have you won something? Come top of your district?"

"Now that's a possibility," he had said. "That is a possibility. I've got some good business this year—it's year-end in three weeks. I canvassed a heap of new customers when those little insurance companies went bust. Umpteen clients

4

came over to me—that's the best about working for a firm like ours—the biggest and best insurance company in the world."

"I bet that's it, then," she had said, rising from the table to start clearing away the breakfast things. "I'll bet you've come top!"

"I'll know tonight," and he had gone through to the office to open the morning's mail.

And Margaret had been right.

At the appointed time, Henry Simmons had walked into the lounge of the Three Tuns Inn, Embleton, and his boss, Charles—"Charlie"—Barnett was already there, sitting on a high stool chatting to the attractive woman at the bar counter.

"Ah, Henry. What'll you have?"

"Pint, please."

"No! Have something stronger! Whisky? What about a whisky—a drop of the hard stuff?"

"All right—you're paying!" and they had laughed. Charlie Barnett had dragged himself away from the woman and had escorted Henry into a quiet corner of the lounge.

"You'll be wondering why I've asked you here, Henry."

"Been puzzling all day," Henry had said. "And so has my wife."

"Got any ideas?"

Henry had shaken his head. He shook it now as he recalled their chat, and the action jerked his mind back to reality—there was a large lorry ahead of him, throwing up a filthy cloud of mud which spattered his windscreen. The wipers had a difficult job clearing it away. He pressed the button of the washers and two tiny jets of water sprayed up from somewhere out of sight; the wipers took over and cleared a space.

He'd have to overtake the lorry. Couldn't sit behind it like this, getting covered in filth and grime.

Henry knew the road ahead—straight and rising slightly; the next dip had a tendency to flood after severe rain, but he didn't think it would be flooded now.

A glance in the mirror. Nothing but

darkness behind. Nothing ahead, beyond the lorry. He eased his vehicle over to its offside in order to peer past the bulky vehicle; his speed had dropped to forty—the legal limit for the lorry.

Henry dropped into third, moved still further into the centre of the road and accelerated past. Its driver flashed his headlights to indicate he knew he was being overtaken; Henry depressed the accelerator still more.

His Hillman responded. The speedometer flickered up to fifty-five and he nicked his dipswitch in acknowledgement of the lorry's signal; he was past.

His speed increased to clear the distance between himself and the lorry; he winked his nearside indicator once to thank the driver for his courtesy and settled down to a steady fifty miles an hour.

The lights of the lorry dwindled behind him as it began a long, steady climb, but his own car maintained its speed on the incline. Two miles further along this road, he must turn left along the valley which took him home.

His mind went back to the pub, back to Charlie Barnett sitting with him at the round table, nursing a double brandy.

"Well, Henry," he had said, "I'm proud of you—at least, I will be at year-end if you continue like this."

"Why? What have I done?" Henry had felt his heart beating excitedly beneath his suit.

"Star Man!" said Barnett. "Star Man. You are leading the field."

"Me? With a country area? You must be joking—there's plenty of agents in urban areas who've surely got more Industrial policies than I have."

"They should have, but they haven't, Henry. You are leading the field at this stage—you are leading the field in the entire north of England, too. I am proud of you; the District Manager is chuffed to bits and the company want to do you proud—if you come out top."

"But . . . Star Man!"

"We've never had one in this district

while I've been here, Henry. We've had men who've come top in one of the branches—Ordinary Branch, General Branch or Industrial Branch, but never top in all three. Until now."

"That means being wined and dined in London, doesn't it?"

"Star treatment, Henry. And you've got just under a month left. You must keep at it. Get among your customers and clients. Do some frantic selling of policies —never mind collecting premiums for the next week or so. Canvas around and get some policies in. Plenty of big 'uns—a few Endowment policies, Life Insurances, that sort of thing. Bit of value to them. See if you can talk some of your farming friends into taking out All-Cover risk for their farm—flog that Diseases of Animals clause and tell 'em about the brucellosis risks."

"OK. I'm on. Think I'll do it?"

"You're well ahead now, Henry. But I don't want you to relax. . . . I want you to know that you are well in the lead, but there are others who'd desperately like to get a Star Man award, Henry. Not locally, but nationally."

"I'll have another whisky," Henry had said. "What about you?"

"Double brandy again?"

"My pleasure," Henry had said.

And so they'd stayed until closing time, basking in their reflected glory, and Henry knew that this was far above anything that had so far happened to him during his work as a rural insurance agent.

He left the pub feeling happy and cheerful; Margaret would be delighted and proud of him, and it would compensate for all his hard work.

And now, he was driving home to tell Margaret the good news, fully aware of the fact that he had had a shade more to drink than was good for him.

He wasn't drunk; nothing like that.

The junction was just ahead on his nearside. He reduced speed, splashed through a wide puddle which spread almost across the road, and flicked the indicator switch.

10

The winking orange light clearly showed his intention and he positioned the car for its turn to the left. Behind him, some lights crested the brow of a distant hill—it would be that lorry, groaning its way through the night. A mini was coming the other way; Henry dipped his headlights.

Then he was round. Off the main road and driving along the narrow lane which led into his village some four miles away. A narrow, twisting lane which he knew like the back of his hand. He'd known it since childhood, riding his bike along here as a schoolboy, racing his mates to the main road, and then racing them back home.

A familiar road; a pleasant road. A quiet road.

Henry didn't like main roads, whether they were "main roads" by country standards or main roads by motorway standards. All of them carried heavy and fast traffic; they sported careless drivers and dangerous drivers. He didn't like that.

He preferred the peace of a rural lane

and he was pleased that his job allowed him to use such pleasant byways.

He was passing the familiar landmarks now. That bungalow on the left which had been empty for so long and which was now occupied by people he'd never seen.

Customers, maybe? Potential life policies?

It was out of his agency; he daren't poach upon a neighbour's territory, not even for one little policy to carry him a step nearer to the elusive Star Man honours.

The farm on the right, set on a high field; a watersplash, running fast from the hills around, its water heading to the cold greyness of the North Sea. All familiar sights. All pleasing for him. All savouring of home.

He looked at his watch, holding his wrist high to catch a reflection from his headlights. Twenty-five past eleven.

Later than he'd thought.

Would Margaret sit up for him? He guessed she would, for she had been just an anxious as he to learn the news from Charlie Barnett.

She was a wonderful woman, was Margaret. A wonderful mother to his two children, Christopher and Joan.

He restored his hand to the steering-wheel and concentrated on the road ahead. The last few miles.

That tricky corner next. It swung to the left, sharp and dangerous in icy weather. Treacherous in snow, but not fearsome to Henry Simmons. Not any more. Not tonight.

Nothing was coming the other way; he would have seen lights through the bare hedgerows. But there were no lights. The road was clear.

He drove into the bend, clinging to the nearside verge, his wheels cutting through the water which lay about the edges. It hissed against the bodywork of his car. His lights moved with him, swinging across the hedges, picking out heavy boughs and dark gaps; reflecting from the eyes of a sheep or a cow or possibly a prowling fox which stared at him through the leafless twigs.

On his left, that old green barn, at the side of the rough farm road which led to a homestead about a mile from the road.

A bad exit in daylight, but all right at night because of vehicle lighting.

He was round.

His lights touched momentarily upon a car parked in that farm entrance; a car without lights.

Blue.

With a dark green mudguard, dented. Hastily repaired. A Jaguar.

He smiled to himself. A courting couple. Lucky devils! It must be nice to be young.

Then a cyclist ahead of him.

Right in the middle of the road.

2

HENRY braked and swung the wheel first one way, then another. The car rocked; tyres screeched on the wet road and the hapless cyclist glanced around. He wobbled violently—it seemed to take an age, but it was all happening at once. All happening together. Unavoidably happening.

The white, terrified face of the cyclist. Henry's shouts. The violently swaying car. Screaming tyres. Crazy lights.

Then the impact.

The thud of the offside wing against the cycle; the rending sound of metal, the crashing of a human body against the bonnet of his car and the crunch of his vehicle as it came to a shuddering halt against the steep grass verge on the far side of the lane.

Then silence. Utter stillness. Not a murmur.

Henry stirred; he had banged his forehead against the windscreen, and there was a trickle of blood running down his cheek. He wiped it off with his hand; his headlights shone into the hedge bottom, two brilliant circles of orange among the grass and dead leaves only inches away from them.

"The bloody fool!" he cursed. "Riding without a rear light!"

He reached for the door handle; must get out and see how that man was.

But the door wouldn't open. The offside of his car was rammed deep into the bank, so he slid across and clambered out of the passenger side.

The cycle was lying nearby, the rear wheel still crazily spinning in the darkness.

No lights on the bike.

The rider?

Henry couldn't see him. Must find him. He began to stagger around the scene, peering into the gloom and then he heard a groan, somewhere near the front of his car.

He moved around, anxiously staring into the darkness. Then that haunted face. Blood spattered. Trapped under the front bumper of the car where it had rammed the verge.

Blood . . . flowing blood. . . .

"God!" and Henry felt weak. "Oh, God! What have I done. . . ?"

He bent down, hands seeking the man underneath. Touched him. The man was groaning softly, all the time. A long, persistent moan; a moan of intense and inescapable pain.

"Got to get him out . . . reverse the car."

Henry got up and ran to the open door. But if he reversed, the car might drop back onto the man and cause more damage. The bumper was wedged into the soft earth which had lifted it a few inches; if he moved it, the car would descend onto the injured man.

Nobody around.

That Jaguar! He suddenly remembered the Jaguar which was parked in the entrance to the farm, only yards along the road. It hadn't come to help. Too bloody wrapped up in themselves to bother about other people!

He ran to get their help.

But the Jaguar's engine was running. He could hear it above the noise of his own urgent panting. It was moving. Thank God! Lights suddenly pierced the gloom of that gateway; twin headlights, moving out.

"Hey!" cried Henry, as the car began to glide out of the gateway. But it turned away from him, away into the gloom. It was going the other way! It accelerated swiftly and left him standing helpless and almost speechless in the roadway.

"You swine!" he cried after it. "You callous swine. You must have known!"

Number! Get its number.

400!

He saw the figures 4–0–0; nothing else. Then it was gone.

"Oh my God!" He found himself shivering. It would be the shock, the aftermath of the accident which was taking effect, so he hurried to his own car. The man was still groaning.

Henry hadn't a torch with him either. No light to see just how serious were his wounds, or how firmly he was trapped. He bent down and whispered, "Got to get you out, my friend. Just got to. I'll manage it somehow."

The man didn't reply; he merely groaned softly, continuously; blood was oozing from somewhere beneath the man's head. Dark, thick blood.

Henry got down to his knees in an effort to examine the extent of the victim's injuries, but it was no good. Beneath the vehicle was a cold black void and the only illumination came from his headlights. And they were firmly wedged into that useless position, staring aimlessly into grass and soft wet earth.

Then a car.

Coming towards him.

Must halt it.

It drew closer and slowed on its approach to the accident. Henry ran into the road.

"Thank God!" he breathed. "Thank God."

In no time at all, police cars and an ambulance were on the scene. In what seemed a matter of minutes, it was all over; the injured man had been whisked off to hospital in the ambulance with a flashing blue light, and Henry's car had been removed to a safe position and now bore side lights only.

A policeman came across to him.

"Now, sir," he began, "are you the driver of that car?"

"Yes—he hadn't any lights on his bike . . . I couldn't avoid him . . . he was in the middle of the road . . ."

"All right. We'll see about that later. Now. Your name, please."

The policeman was pulling a notebook from his pocket. Henry saw the words "Accident Report Book" in heavy print across the front.

"Henry Simmons."

The policeman opened the book and started to write down Henry's particulars.

"Address?"

"Hive Cottage, Drydale."

"Age?"

"Thirty-three."

"Occupation?"

"Insurance Agent."

"Driving licence?"

Henry took out his wallet and passed the licence and his certificate of insurance to the policeman who jotted particulars in his booklet.

"The cyclist. How is he?" Henry asked nervously.

"He's very seriously injured, Mr. Simmons. Very seriously. He's got a severe head wound and a fractured right leg. We also suspect internal injuries. He got one hell of a knock, you know."

Henry didn't reply. There was nothing he could say.

"Now," the policeman said solemnly, "before we go any further, I have reason to think you have been drinking."

"Drinking? You don't think. . . ."

The policeman interrupted him. "It is

my duty to ask if you will take the breathalyser test, Mr. Simmons."

"But . . . he had no lights! He was wobbling down the middle. . . ."

"You are not obliged to say anything, Mr. Simmons, and if you take my advice, you will keep quiet about what happened. Now, the breath test."

"But it wasn't my fault!"

"That doesn't matter. Will you allow me to take one?"

"Oh God!" Henry recalled the drinks he'd had with Charlie Barnett; the whiskies. What time was it now?

He glanced at his watch. Nearly midnight.

Hell—how time flew!

He nodded. He would take the breath test. There was no alternative.

The policeman went to his mini-van, still with its blue light flashing, and returned with the little green box of breathalysers.

Henry felt like running away; suppose he refused to take one? What would they do then?

They'd arrest him—he knew that.

The policeman was taking one of the little glass tubes out of the box, and he pushed the pointed ends into the side of the green container and snapped off its sealed ends. Then he fitted a rubber mouthpiece at one end, and a clear plastic bag at the other.

"Now," he said, "you blow that bag up."

"Do I have to?"

"You can be arrested if you don't."

Henry took the device; his hands shook visibly but the policeman said nothing, merely looking on, solemn-faced and impassive.

Henry blew. He found it difficult due to the narrow opening of the glass tube, but soon he had the plastic bag swelling with his breath.

After what seemed an age, the policeman nodded, "That'll do," and Henry passed the bag back to him, wondering about the result.

He found himself thinking of Margaret.

"Positive," grunted the policeman, and

he stared at Henry with an unsmiling face. "Positive, Mr. Simmons. You've had too much to drink and you've run down a pedal cyclist."

"Oh, my God!" and Henry felt faint. "Are you sure it's positive?"

"See for yourself," and the policeman showed Henry the little tube of crystals; they had turned green above the line which indicated the prescribed limit. "Green. Henry Simmons. I must inform you that you are now under arrest for driving a motor vehicle on a road with more than the prescribed amount of alcohol in your body. You are not obliged to say anything unless you wish to do so but what you say may be taken down in writing and given in evidence."

"Can I ring my wife?"

"When we get to the office. Come along. One of our men will drive your car to Embleton police station—it's not badly damaged. We'll complete details of the accident there."

Drunken driving! What if the cyclist died?

"Go and sit in my van," ordered the policeman. "Got any valuables in your car?"

Henry shook his head.

They were taking him away; he was under arrest! Him. Henry Simmons. Under arrest for drunken driving, and he'd knocked a pedal cyclist off his machine into the bargain!

He saw his policeman; he was talking to another one who was measuring the road with a long tape measure and then his policeman returned.

"PC Ford will drive your car, and the beat van will fetch that bike. Made a mess of that, haven't you?"

"Are you trying to catch me out?" demanded Henry, angrily alert.

"Sorry I spoke," and the policeman started the engine of his mini-van, turned it around and drove off towards Embleton with Henry beside him.

Margaret looked at the clock for the hundredth time. Quarter past twelve.

She paced up and down the room.

Henry must have had an accident. He must. He would never be as late as this without letting her know, not unless something had happened—perhaps he was at Mr. Barnett's house.

Ought she to ring?

It was very late and if Henry was there, she would look a bit silly. And yet something could have happened to him.

She would ring.

She dialled Barnett's number and his telephone rang for a long, long time. Was Barnett throwing a party? Was Henry there with him . . . with . . . another woman? No, not Henry. Surely not. . . .

The telephone was still ringing, and then someone picked it up.

"Barnett," said a thick, tired voice. She'd probably got him out of bed.

"Mr. Barnett . . . this is Margaret Simmons."

"Who? Oh, yes. Henry's wife. Why are you ringing? Something wrong?"

"Henry hasn't come home, Mr. Barnett. I wondered if he was still with you."

"Henry?" the voice was suddenly alert. "Not home? He was with me until nearly eleven. Are you sure he's not home?"

"Positive. I thought he might be at your house."

"No, he's not here. Must have broken down. What time is it?"

"Quarter past twelve."

"I'll ring the police to see if they've heard anything. There might have been an accident or something."

"Accident!" shrieked Margaret Simmons.

"Henry might have stopped to help—you never know. Now, don't worry. I'll ring you back in a minute."

Accident! She replaced the receiver. No. Not Henry.

She went upstairs to have a look at the children. They were her next thought.

"Sit down there," ordered the policeman. "The doctor's coming."

"Doctor?"

"To take a blood sample from you. We want to have it analysed."

"Can I have my own doctor?"

"If you like."

"And my solicitor?"

"If you like."

"You'll ring them?"

"I will. Give me their names."

Henry told the policeman who scribbled down the names, and the policeman said, "Don't look so agitated, Mr. Simmons. We get a lot of motorists here due to the initial test with the breathalyser and the laboratory analysis of their blood or urine often proves negative. You're obviously a border line case, so stop worrying."

"Stop worrying! How the hell can I? Look at the pickle I'm in!"

"You are, aren't you? Now, before we do anything else, you have the opportunity to take another breath test here, in the police station. The law says so. How about it?"

"And if it's negative?"

"We take no further action."

"I'd like to take another."

"Want your solicitor and doctor calling first?"

"No. It doesn't matter. Give me the other test, then I'll decide."

"Good idea. You're not obliged to take this one, you know. It's a sort of bonus. If it is positive, we'll need a blood sample or a urine sample from you."

"That's fair enough."

The telephone rang, and the policeman answered it. "Embleton Police Office."

Henry tried not to listen, but the policeman looked down at him and said, "Yes, he's here. Would you like to speak to him?"

Margaret!

"There's a Mr. Barnett on the phone —he'd like to speak to you," and Henry took the receiver.

"Simmons," he announced himself.

"Henry! What in the name of God's happened? Your wife's as worried as hell —got me out of bed."

"There was an accident, Mr. Barnett. A cyclist. I knocked him down . . . he had no lights. I didn't stand a chance."

"How is he?"

"He was taken to hospital."

"What are you doing there?"

Henry paused, then said, "They're giving me the breathalyser."

"Oh my God!" moaned Barnett. "What shall I tell your wife?"

"Just say I was involved in a slight accident—I'm not hurt and will be home as soon as I can."

"Right. Want any help?"

"No, I'm all right."

"Shall I come over? I live only a mile away."

"If you like," and Henry looked at the waiting policeman, who had been assembling another breathalyser. He didn't say anything.

"I'll come, then, Henry."

"You'll ring Margaret first?"

"Of course," and the line went dead.

"Right," said the policeman. "If Mr. Barnett comes in, he mustn't interrupt what we're doing or saying. I know him. Your boss, is he?"

"Yes. I was with him earlier tonight.

My wife rang him to find out where I was."

"Right. Here. Blow this one up now."

Henry repeated the performance with the second breathalyser and the watchful policeman stood over him; Henry passed the balloon-like bag to him, heart thumping.

"Hmm," he grunted, peering at the crystals beneath the light in the office. "Look. Negative this time. Border line, though. Fair enough, Mr. Simmons. That satisfies me."

"Is that all then?"

"So far as any allegation of drunken driving is concerned, you have no need to fear. Now, I've got some questions about the accident. You said the cyclist hadn't any lights."

"He had no lights at all. I'm sure of that."

"Would it have made any difference if he had?"

"I don't know. I think I'd have seen a red light glowing in the distance— through the bare hedges. But he was in the middle of the road . . . wobbling all over."

"Any proof?"

"Proof?"

"Proof that he was in the middle of the road without lights."

"Well, no. I haven't any proof."

"You'll need some."

"Won't my word do?"

"I inspected that bike, Mr. Simmons, when it was lying in the road. It had lights fitted. Battery lights, front and rear."

"But they weren't on, were they?"

"They were broken with the impact. When the bike is brought in, you'll see for yourself."

"But what can I do?"

"Nothing. There were no witnesses, I take it?"

"No one," said Henry. Then he remembered the blue Jaguar in the gateway. "Wait, there was a Jaguar. It was parked in that farm entrance just before the scene of the accident. It had no lights on. The cyclist must have ridden past the gateway only seconds before. . . ."

"Jaguar?"

"Yes. A blue one with a repaired mudguard."

"Didn't they come to help you?"

"No. I went back to ask them but they drove away in the opposite direction—towards Embleton in fact."

"Local car?"

"I've never seen it before. I couldn't see the number—except it had 400 in it."

"They just drove away?" the policeman sounded puzzled.

"Yes. But they must have heard the crash and seen lights go astray . . . they must. They were only yards away."

"They?"

"Well, whoever was in the Jag."

"OK. I'll need a written statement from you giving every detail. Speed?"

"Fortyish."

"Weather?"

"Terrible. You saw it for yourself."

"Familiar with that road."

"Used it all my life."

"Right. Let's start to get it written down." Footsteps sounded in the entrance to the police station and the policeman paused to see who was coming. "It might be our lot back from the scene."

It wasn't.

It was Charlie Barnett who strode to the counter and as he recognized his colleague, the telephone rang.

"Embleton Police—PC Christian speaking," answered the officer.

He listened, grim-faced, then put down the telephone.

"That was the hospital," he said. "The cyclist has died."

3

FOR PC Joe Christian, the man who had interviewed Henry Simmons, the accident was, so far, fairly routine. He had taken a statement from Simmons, and his colleagues had investigated the scene.

The cycle had been brought to the police office, and there were lamps attached to the front and rear. The question was—had the cycle borne illuminated lights, particularly the rear light, at the time of the accident?

PC Christian could not decide that. The decision would lie with the Court. Christian had warned Simmons of the possibility that he would be prosecuted for dangerous, reckless or careless driving, and had said the charge might even amount to one of causing death by dangerous driving.

Simmons had left the office at quarter

to one, driven home by his boss, Charlie Barnett. His damaged car had been brought to the police station and Simmons left it there to be repaired at a local garage in due course.

At 2 a.m. PC Joe Christian made his way to the hospital. He was already working overtime—he should have finished duty at one o'clock.

At the reception desk he asked for the doctor on Casualty, and was taken to see Dr. Forshaw.

"Good morning, doctor. Nasty business, that cyclist. Where is he?"

"In the mortuary. You'll want to see him?"

"Please. Who is he?"

"No idea."

"Oh, crumbs! Don't say we've got an unidentified corpse on our hands, doctor!"

"It looks like it. Our staff removed all his clothes and there's nothing in them to say who he is."

"What were his injuries?"

"Multiple is the official description.

Severe fracture at the base of his skull; some brain damage, I'd say. Lots of other fractures—ribs, right leg, right arm. Some internal injuries as well, but we won't be sure of their nature until the post mortem."

"Fair enough. Right, can we go to the morgue now?"

Dr. Forshaw escorted PC Christian along the tiled corridors, turned right at the distant end and together they descended to the hospital mortuary, a clean, clinically fresh place set apart from the main building.

Forshaw unlocked it and switched on the light.

"Over there."

Joe Christian looked in the direction indicated and saw the body lying face uppermost on the white slab. The wounds had been cleaned.

"Not an old chap," muttered Christian. "Middle thirties, eh?"

"That's about right," commented Dr. Forshaw.

"Was he clean when he was brought in?"

"Oh, yes. Not a tramp, or a filthy character at all. Very clean and well groomed. Look at his hands—not rough, are they? Nails well kept too."

"Mmm. Heavy build—fourteen stone mark?"

"I'd say so, Mr. Christian. Well nourished. Healthy character in life by the look of him."

Joe Christian took a tape measure from his uniform pocket and measured the body.

"Five feet eleven inches—tall chap. Brown hair. Got his own teeth. Grey eyes. Fresh complexion. No scars, are there? Operation scars, I mean."

"Nothing," confirmed Dr. Forshaw. "We had a good look."

"Fairly nondescript sort of character, isn't he?"

"I'm afraid so. Looks as though you've got a job on your hands now. What'll you do about getting him identified?"

"Hard to say. If he's a local character

—which you'd expect him to be—someone will be shouting about eight o'clock this morning. You don't expect visitors to be riding about on bikes, do you? Logically, he'll be a local chap going home from work, or from the pub, or from seeing his girl friend. But there are no pubs within reasonable cycling distance of where he was killed. Might be a girl somewhere. Simmons did mention a blue Jaguar . . . rich girl friend?"

"Pardon?"

"Sorry. I was thinking aloud. The chap who knocked him down said there was a blue Jaguar parked in a gateway only yards from the scene, but it drove off without helping. I was wondering if this chap had been secretly meeting some wealthy girl friend. You know—her Ladyship and the Gamekeeper type of relationship."

"I suppose it's feasible. She'd drive off because she didn't want to be recognized."

"That's a good theory, doctor. I'll follow that one up—the press might help to get him identified. We shouldn't have any difficulty if he is a local chap."

"Have you any description of the Jaguar?"

"Not really. Simmons thought it was blue with a damaged front wing, and he saw the figures 400 in the registration plate. That's not enough for us to trace it through taxation records, although our chaps might come across it somewhere. But he might be mistaken about those figures—it was dark and raining. Still, we've taken particulars and we'll circulate it."

"Can't say I know it. Now, back to our friend here. Anything else you want?"

"His clothes. I'll have to search them, and take them away. Then we'll have to inform the coroner."

"Will you do that?"

"Yes, first thing in the morning. He'll demand a post-mortem without any doubt."

"We can do it here. His clothes will be in No. 3 locker in the ante-room."

PC Christian was shown to the locker,

and with the doctor he examined the clothing.

"An old raincoat. Navy blue. That would make him hard to see, wouldn't it?" Christian commented, searching its pockets. There were two or three cigarette ends and a pair of old brown leather gloves. He listed them in his notebook.

"Fairly dry, too. Wet at the back, but dry elsewhere. And it was pouring down. Laid on the wet road . . . dry because he was in that Jaguar? It's a possibility— when did it start to rain?"

"Uh . . . ten o'clock, or thereabouts."

"Mmm . . . jacket, Harris tweed, good condition. Pockets . . . one ball-point pen, blue; wallet, brown leather, fold-over type, containing one Bank of England one pound note, a ten shilling note, six fourpenny postage stamps. Nothing else. Other pockets . . . empty."

Dr. Forshaw passed over the trousers.

"Cavalry twill—fawn, also wet at the back and on one leg. Handkerchief, cash. How much?" and Christian counted it out. "Seven and ninepence. Doesn't believe in carrying much cash, does he?"

He continued to search the trousers, "Comb; pocket knife; piece of string; pencil sharpener."

"No cigarettes," noticed the doctor.

"A good point," added Christian. "And that's all his personal property. String vest, underpants, socks and shoes . . . almost dry. No tie; coloured shirt with collar attached."

"It's all good quality clothing, isn't it?"

"I agree, doctor. He's not the sort of man you'd expect to be riding a bike, is he?"

"Far from it. Now, you'll want a signature for this, won't you?"

"Please. There's nothing I can do here, doctor. I'll have the coroner informed first thing in the morning, and we'll fix a post-mortem here. My job is to have this chap identified, and that will be done through our official channels."

"Right. You let me know—how you go on, I mean. He'll have to be buried, you know."

"Of course. He'll keep in the fridge for a week or two, won't he?"

"If necessary."

And they left the mortuary.

Mr. and Mrs. Henry Simmons sat late into the night. Henry had told Margaret all about his Star Man achievement and then about the accident.

"But Henry, they must trace that Jaguar, mustn't they? Otherwise how will they know you're telling the truth?"

"But they'll never find it, darling," persisted Henry. "They can't. I didn't get its number. Part of a number is no use to the police."

"But surely it must be some use?"

"Charlie Barnett said he'd send a description of it to all our local chaps."

"Charlie Barnett? Why's he taken such a sudden interest in you?"

"He wants me to win the Star Man award. He's thinking of his own prestige, but at least our chaps are out and about all day, and they do know a lot of people, Margaret."

"Suppose the car is traced?"

"The police will interview the driver. Ask him what he saw."

"Darling, I'm sorry," and Margaret put her arms about her husband. "I do hope he's traced."

"If not, I'll be hauled before the magistrates charged with careless driving at the least, or even dangerous driving. That would be disastrous."

"You'd lose your licence?"

"More than likely. And a lost licence means no work for me."

"But at least you weren't injured, darling. That's all that matters to me. Come along, Henry. Time for bed. Let's try to get some sleep."

"It won't be easy," said Henry Simmons.

Shortly after nine o'clock that same morning, the coroner was informed and he ordered a post-mortem examination. By now, a verbal description of the dead man had been circulated to all local police stations, and a photograph had been sent to Scotland Yard and to the regional Clearing Houses for normal distribution through routine police publications.

The man in charge of Embleton Police Division, Superintendent Jack Harris, strode into his office at 9.15 a.m., and first demanded the Occurrence Book as was his daily practice.

He read all about the events which had occurred during the night, and paid special attention to PC Christian's report of the fatal accident.

Christian was a good policeman. Experienced and thorough, with ten years' service. Harris read the account carefully, looking for procedural routines which had been overlooked, for he bore the overall responsibility for the efficiency of his division.

He spoke to the duty Inspector who hovered in his office as he read the daily events; the Inspector was always there to answer queries.

"Christian gave the driver a breath-alyser, eh?"

"First one positive, sir, but the second

was negative. And he wasn't drunk enough to be charged under the old procedure—Section 6, Road Traffic Act 1960."

"Fair enough. Is Simmons being charged with causing death by dangerous driving?"

"Quite possibly, sir, but he alleges the cyclist had no lights."

"They all say that, Inspector. If he'd been drinking, it wouldn't matter whether the poor cyclist had ten lights. Seems a good 'Death by Dangerous' to me. The lights—were there any on the bike?"

"Battery lamps, front and rear. Both smashed in the accident."

"Pity. Witnesses?"

"No independent witnesses. But Simmons—the driver—did report a car nearby."

"I've seen that bit. Are we trying to trace it?"

"We've circulated particulars."

"What about fingerprinting that corpse, Inspector? Has that been done?"

"Fingerprinting, sir?"

"Yes. Common sense, surely."

"Er, no. It hasn't been done."

"Then I think it should be. Fix that, will you—there should be someone in CID now. Get them up to the hospital immediately."

"Yes, sir."

"Now, this complaint from old Mrs. Smithers. Those bloody dogs barking all night again. . . ."

"I've sent Wilkinson along to see the owner of the dogs."

And so the routine work of the Embleton police got underway for yet another day.

Margaret Simmons pleaded with her husband. "But Mr. Barnett said it would be all right to take a day off work, Henry."

"I'm all right, Margaret. It'll be better for me to get on with some work. Besides, I'm going to be the Star Man— remember?"

"But you've got no car."

"It'll be fixed in a day or so. The garage

said it wouldn't take long to knock out a few dents in the front. In the meantime, I can walk; I can go to neighbouring villages on the bus."

"You seem determined. . . ."

"I'd get myself into an awful state if I sat around all day doing nothing."

"Who is the . . . the dead man?" Margaret tried to put the question delicately.

"They didn't know last night. I'll ring them now. I might go and see his relatives."

"Do you think that's wise?"

"Why not? It wasn't my fault." He almost shouted the words.

"Ring them now," said Margaret quietly, turning away to clear the breakfast table. "The police, I mean."

Henry went through to the room he used as an office, and returned in a few moments, shaking his head. "They still don't know who he is."

Margaret said nothing, but worked quietly with the breakfast things.

"I won't be in for lunch," Henry said.

"Want sandwiches?"

"No. I'll go over to Renwick—their pub puts on good snacks. I can get the bus in twenty minutes."

"All right," Margaret said. "What time will you be in?"

"Tea-time. Just after five."

"Bye," and he kissed her on the cheek.

It was about this time that the breakfast-room waitress at the Grapes Inn, Stilling, tapped on the manager's door. Stilling was about six miles away from Henry's house.

"Come," he shouted as he sorted through the morning's mail.

The waitress, a slim freckled girl called Irene, padded in and stood before him.

"Well?" he didn't look up from the mail; a gaunt, miserable-faced individual called Henderson.

"The man in No. 7, Mr. Henderson. He hasn't been down for breakfast."

"Has anyone knocked?"

"Dorothy has but he didn't answer."

"I'll go."

49

Henderson dragged himself from his chair with a weary sigh and, on the way, grabbed a spare key to bedroom No. 7.

Either the guest had overslept, or he had gone without paying. Both were only too common these days.

With Irene at his side, Henderson knocked loudly on the door of the room. "What's his name?" he whispered.

"Mr. Cosford."

"Mr. Cosford," shouted Henderson. "Are you there?" Nothing.

He waited, then tried again. He achieved the same result.

"I'll go in," and he inserted the key in the lock and opened the door.

Irene followed him inside; the room was empty.

"Bed not slept in, Irene," grunted Henderson. "Suitcase still here . . . funny."

"Has he done us, Mr. Henderson?"

"Looks like it, Irene. Lock it up—I'll ring the police."

PC Christian came on duty at ten o'clock,

his face paler than usual after his late night. He arrived to find that the coroner had ordered a post-mortem which was to be performed at the hospital at eleven thirty that morning.

Superintendent Harris had ordered the deceased's fingerprints to be taken and this had been done by the CID; already the prints were in the post, en route to Scotland Yard for comparison with their records. There was always a possibility the man had a criminal record.

As Joe Christian busied himself in the office, catching up with the latest progress of the fatal accident, the telephone rang. He answered it.

"Henderson speaking, Grapes Inn, Stilling," announced the caller.

"Yes, Mr. Henderson. PC Christian here. What's bothering you."

"Another guest sneaked off without paying—except this one's left his suit-case."

"What name did he give?"

"Cosford. He signed our register as Mr.

B. Cosford, Flat 27B, Osbourne House, Princes Avenue, Leeds."

"Thanks. What did he look like?"

From the description given, Joe Christian knew that the missing guest was now lying dead in Embleton Hospital Mortuary.

"I'll come over to see you, Mr. Henderson," he said.

Within half-an-hour, Cosford's luggage had been searched, but it contained little of interest. There was nothing to establish or confirm his identity; the suitcase contained a change of underclothing and some toilet requisites.

Joe Christian told Henderson about the fatal accident, and left the inn with the luggage and personal effects. He promised to ring back with details of next-of-kin, because Henderson was owed two night's lodgings.

Back at the office, with half-an-hour to spare before his attendance at the post-mortem examination, PC Christian rang Leeds City Police and asked them to deliver a message to the address given in the Grapes Inn register. He asked that the relatives be notified of the death, and that one of them contact him with a view to arrange the funeral and the other necessities of sudden death.

The post-mortem was a formality—the pathologist found that Cosford's heart and lungs had been in first class condition, and his injuries were consistent with being knocked down by a motor vehicle travelling at speed. His injuries were found to be a fractured skull, a fractured base of the spine, damage to the brain and a few minor fractures. Death was probably due to shock following the injuries, but the brain damage was beyond repair. It was a blessing the man had died.

Joe Christian returned to the office with his information which would be passed to the coroner. The office duty man had a message for him.

"From Leeds City—that address you gave for Cosford. It doesn't exist, Joe."

4

"**F**ALSE address?"

"There's no such address in Leeds and they've checked on the voters' lists. There's only one B. Cosford —that name was checked and it was a woman—Barbara Cosford, who is nearly seventy and a spinster. She's never heard of your victim, Joe."

"That would bloody well happen, wouldn't it? I thought it was too good to be true. Nothing's simple any more, is it? What now?"

"Back to square one. You've still got an unidentified body on your hands."

"And something else by the look of it. I'll have to go back and see that hotel manager. The boss is sure to ask what I've done about it. You know where to find me."

Joe Christian took one of the station cars and drove to Stilling. He parked in front of the Grapes Inn and hurried inside, hoping that Henderson was there.

He was.

"Back so soon, Mr. Christian?"

"Problems, Mr. Henderson. That character Cosford—he gave you a false address."

"Did he, by Jove! False name, too?"

"We don't know about that until we get more information, but it's a fair chance it isn't his correct name. Now, when did he arrive here?"

"The evening before last—Sunday night. About half-past six."

"How?"

"Car, I expect. There are no buses on Sundays out here."

"Did you see his car?"

"No, but he came in with two other chaps."

"Friends?"

"I think so. They waited until he'd booked in, then they all had dinner. They left here about ten o'clock and he stayed."

"What were they like?"

"I didn't take much notice, quite

frankly, although I was knocking about the place until closing-time. Both youngish chaps—late twenties or early thirties. One was big and tall, the—other was smaller."

"Dress?"

"Dark suits. White shirts, or something very light. Smart chaps. Not the sort you'd notice particularly in a place like this."

"Accents?"

"Like Cosford. Nothing that was noticeable—well spoken chaps, all of them."

"Did you see their car?"

Henderson shook his head.

"Would any of your staff see it?"

"Doubt it. Cars park out front, and our curtains are closed very early during these dark evenings. You can ask the staff if you like."

"I will before I leave."

"Are they crooks then?"

"Dunno, Mr. Henderson. No idea what they're up to. Men give false names for all sorts of reasons—women, business

56

and crime. Nothing suspicious has been reported around here."

"I suppose they could be business men engaged in some secret deal, and covering their tracks," suggested Henderson.

"It's a thought. Anyway, that's all you can say?"

"Yes; sorry I can't help more."

"You've given us a lot of help already, Mr. Henderson. It's our first lead about this dead man. Funny about the bike, though. I wonder where he got that from."

"Might have come from our yard. There are a few lying around at the back of the inn, and none of them have a definite owner. They've been left by people who have never returned. We keep them, and people in the village borrow them. There's about half-a-dozen out there."

"Would you know them?"

"The bikes?"

"Yes. Could you identify them? I'd like to know where the dead man got his bike."

"Come out with me, now. We'll have a look."

Outside, Henderson confirmed that a cycle was missing, and said it was a gent's black one, with no special identifying features.

"What about lights on it?"

"We wouldn't bother with batteries for their lights, if that's what you mean. Some have lamps, as you can see, but I shouldn't think they work."

Christian peered at the assortment of old cycles which lay under cover of the external buildings of this ancient public house.

"Haven't any of them got owners?"

"Not to my knowledge. People ride them as they want—they were here when I came, so I don't bother about them. The customers pump the tyres up and so on— they're a bonus for patrons of the pub!"

"Did Cosford ask to borrow one?"

"Might have asked one of the staff."

"Suppose he'd asked for lights?"

"He'd have been told to buy his own batteries—they're only a few bob."

"Thanks. Will you be in Embleton in the near future?"

"This afternoon, or tomorrow."

"Could you call at the police station and have a look at the bike we've got? It's battered now, but we'd like a positive identification."

"I'll do that, but I don't want that bike back."

"We'll dispose of it, and while you're there, we might want you to view the dead man to identify him as the person known to you as Cosford."

"Right. I'll do that as well. I'm not afraid of dead bodies, you know, not after serving at the front in France."

"Good. Some of our customers are terrified," grinned PC Christian. "If I'm not around when you call, tell the sergeant why you've come. I'll tell him to expect you."

"Anything to help—you chaps have done me a bit of good in my time. Can I get you a drink?"

They were walking back to the public house now, but Christian shook his head.

"Love to," he said, "but I've got to get back."

"Call again," invited Henderson, and PC Christian said he would call when he was off duty. He'd bring his wife, too.

Every insurance agent within Charlie Barnett's jurisdiction received a telephone call from him on this Tuesday morning and he described the Jaguar car to his men. All of them promised to keep an eye open for it, but one or two decided to ignore the request.

They knew why Barnett had done this —he was trying to get Simmons off the hook so that he would win the Star Man award; that would give Barnett a welcome boost in the eyes of the management.

So a few of them just left it at that; if Henry Simmons was daft enough to get himself drunk and then have the gall to kill a cyclist, that was his hard luck. He should have thought about that before going out boozing. Besides, if Simmons was out of work for a while, someone else might get an award for being top of some

Branch—no one could get a Star Man award this year now, apart from Simmons, but a few smaller honours were still open.

So those one or two agents promptly dismissed the request.

The others, however, were interested. They knew and respected Henry Simmons for his personality and his determination to succeed, and each went to work with one eye continually open for a blue Jaguar with a dented wing at the front. They knew that the wing was roughly painted in a green colour, probably an undercoat, and that the registration figures were thought to contain the numbers 400.

One such agent was Jim Kennedy, a youthful man with a pretty wife and a baby girl.

Kennedy had been appointed to his agency eighteen months ago and was keen and industrious; he was alert and the message about the Jaguar intrigued him.

His agency was on the outskirts of a small industrial town, with one or two minor factories and a growing steelworks. It kept him busy.

During the late afternoon of Tuesday, he had paid a visit to a small plastics factory which had recently opened; the manager had been sympathetic, but he hadn't given Kennedy any business.

Afterwards, Kennedy sat in his car, making rough notes of the extent of the plastics business, its buildings and some remarks made to him by the chairman. He was vaguely aware of the traffic which roared past him, heading into the vastness of Tees-side to the north, or along the coast roads towards the south.

Cars, buses, goods-vehicles; workers coming home, workers starting their shifts.

He looked with unseeing eyes at the eternal traffic, whilst making further notes in his book. He would use these comments later, and he'd call again on this factory at a future date.

Then a blue Jaguar. Moving north with the flow of traffic. Away from him; he turned in his seat and stared. Patched mudguard!

A bus blocked his view; Jim Kennedy started his car and reversed into a gateway. His heart was pounding.

He couldn't emerge yet, due to the persistent traffic, and the Jaguar had slowed behind a double-decker bus which was disgorging passengers about fifty yards up the road.

Registration number?

Jim Kennedy couldn't read it. It was too far away. Must follow it.

The double-decker was moving again, drawing slowly away from the stop, and the line of traffic followed suit. Kennedy glanced to his right.

Only a scooter coming. A three-tonner behind it.

Might just make it.

He slammed first gear home and pressed the accelerator; his little Austin leapt forward and he joined the tail end of the queue behind the bus; the scooter nipped past him and the lorry driver flashed his headlights and glared down at the cheeky Austin.

But Kennedy was out and he was in the same queue as the Jaguar. The problem would be keeping it in sight.

Kennedy knew this road well; he knew all its turnings, twists and places to overtake; he knew the short cuts, the back streets and the shopping-centres which lay nearby.

Ahead of him, the double-decker was still at the head of the queue, and there was a bus stop about two hundred yards away; it was off the road, and allowed two buses to stand there, quite apart from the traffic.

At that point also, the road widened and a further mile ahead, there was a main road junction, one road branching into Tees-side and the other heading further north, across the Tees and into County Durham.

If the Jaguar opened up on that road, Kennedy's little Austin wouldn't stand a chance. It would be left standing.

Jim plodded on, keeping an eye on the

pale blue roof ahead of him; clearly the driver of the Jaguar was not rushing and seemed to be taking extreme care not to exceed the speed limit, nor to antagonize other drivers.

In the eyes of Jim Kennedy he drove like a criminal; like a criminal taking every traffic precaution; like a criminal who didn't want to attract the attention of other road users.

But the Jaguar didn't reach the wide portion. It indicated that it was about to make a left turn, and positioned itself for the manoeuvre. Jim did likewise.

Gradually, the blue roof eased towards the nearside of the road, separating itself from the stream of northbound traffic until it eventually detached itself from the line and turned into a minor road. This led into a housing-estate.

A van followed it; it was the baker's van which made a daily round of the estate. Jim Kennedy also filtered left. The Jaguar pulled away and increased speed as it travelled through the avenues of brick-built houses.

The van stopped to serve the first houses; Jim overtook it and was now behind the Jaguar, although some hundred yards away from it.

Nonetheless it was directly ahead of him, but he was still unable to read its registration number.

It continued at a fast speed—approaching forty miles an hour and it seemed to have abandoned the care it had exercised in the thick of the main-road traffic. Perhaps this was due to the comparative peace of this estate.

Then its brake lights showed red against its blue body; it was slowing near a large house which stood in its own grounds on a junction ahead of him. An expensive house with a double garage.

But the Jaguar did not turn into the driveway of the house; it merely parked outside on the road. Two men got out.

Jim drew up behind it. By now the men had disappeared into the house.

Jim took his notebook from the dashboard shelf and examined the registration plate of the car he'd followed. PDF40Q.

Not 400 as Henry Simmons had thought. But such a mistake was easily made in the dark. "Q" might well look like "O". He jotted the number in the book, then pushed it back into place beneath the dashboard.

The house.

What was the name of this house?

Jim got out of his car and walked towards it; beneath his arm he carried his collecting-book, and in the other hand, his brief case. He wanted to look like an insurance agent doing his rounds.

The entrance to the large house was at an angle to the road, and he couldn't see the name or number. But a walk past it would enable him to get the information he wanted.

Jim Kennedy found himself getting excited; he looked about him anxiously, wondering if he looked like an ordinary man doing an ordinary job.

The estate was quiet; one or two women were out and about, some pushing prams on afternoon walks, or returning from one of the local shopping-centres.

School children were rushing home after their day's lessons and one or two workmen were moving off, to start their evening shift.

Jim felt he wouldn't be conspicuous.

He was level with the parked Jaguar.

He stopped briefly to look at it. Light blue with a dark green front offside wing, badly dented. Nice condition otherwise. A briefcase on the front passenger seat. A newspaper—*The Times*—in the rear.

Nothing else of note.

He passed on, turning right as the footpath veered away. For a moment he paused before the grand house. On the white metal gates, there was the number 28.

No name.

"What's the name of this road?" he muttered to himself and turned around to seek a street name-plate. But there wasn't one, not at this junction.

There would be one somewhere.

As he turned on his heels, he spotted a telephone kiosk and decided to ring his boss; but first he must know the name of the road.

The kiosk! It would be given on the notices inside the kiosk, and so he crossed the road towards the call box and entered it.

The door closed behind him and he put his briefcase and collecting-book on the floor, then sought the identifying position of the kiosk.

He found it. A printed notice said, "This kiosk is at Almond Grove, Southburn. The number is Southburn 2112."

"Almond Grove," he made a mental note of the name. Now he'd ring Charlie Barnett.

He dialled the requisite number on the STD, and it wasn't long before Charlie Barnett's familiar voice responded.

Jim pressed a sixpence into the box and spoke.

"Jim Kennedy here, Mr. Barnett."

"Yes, Jim. You're ringing from a kiosk. I heard the pips. Something wrong?"

"You're sharp today," commented Jim. "It's outside No. 28 Almond Grove, Southburn."

"What is?"

"That blue Jaguar . . . it's. . . ."

Then the kiosk door opened behind him. A large hand grabbed the telephone and slammed the mouthpiece down on the rest.

Then a voice said, "Out of there, mister."

5

"**H**EY!" shouted Jim "What's the idea?"

"Out!" said the man standing in the open door.

"Come on. No funny business."

"Look. I was making a phone call. . . ."

"I heard you. Out!"

Jim Kennedy stood his ground and turned completely round in the confined space. There was another man; they were the men who had driven the Jaguar to this place.

"If you don't allow me to make my call, I will get the police." Jim spoke softly, but there was a noticeable tremor in his voice.

"That's just what we don't want you to do," and the front one produced a tiny snub-nosed automatic from the pocket of his suit. "So you are coming with us."

Jim swallowed. The man's eyes were cold and hard, and he held the little pistol dangerously steady.

"Come on, mister. Out you come."

Jim thought of his wife; his baby girl; the man reached out with his free hand and took hold of Jim's arm.

"I'll come. No need for that," and reluctantly Jim Kennedy stepped out of the kiosk. The man seized Jim's briefcase and collecting-book.

"Into the Jaguar," snapped his captor. "We want a talk with you."

Jim said nothing; he walked steadily away with the man walking close to him. The second man remained a step or two behind.

Two men. Early thirties. One slightly taller than the other.

As they neared the car, the shorter of the two rushed forward to open the rear door and Jim was pushed towards it; he clambered unwillingly inside and the man with the gun sat beside him.

"Right, Bill," said the man. "Drive us around for a bit, will you?"

Bill, the shorter of the two, took the driver's seat and started the car. It moved forward, turned right at the junction, then sped away.

As it drove, Jim looked straight ahead; the man had the nozzle of the tiny pistol pressed into Jim's ribs, pressing so that it hurt through his clothing.

"Right, mister. Look at me. Who are you?"

Jim didn't answer. He continued to look straight ahead, but his eyes were unseeing. Who were these men?

"All right. We've got your belongings."

The man relaxed his pressure with the gun.

"Don't try to get out of the car," he snapped, reaching for the briefcase. He rested it on his knee and opened it.

"Mmm," he said as he searched it. "Insurance agent, eh? That's funny, isn't it, Bill?"

The driver laughed aloud; a hearty, cruel laugh.

"That's our business too, mister. Now, your name . . . ah! Here we are.

73

Kennedy. James Kennedy, 47 Iburndale Terrace, Crafton. Now we know your name and we know your address. That's nice. We can insure you now."

"What do you want?" demanded Jim, thinking again of his wife and child. He looked at the man beside him; the car was driving round and round the estate. Jim was lost already.

"Your co-operation, Mr. Kennedy."

"No," snapped Jim.

"Drive into the country, Bill," said the man beside Jim Kennedy, and he made Jim sink deep into the car; he couldn't be seen, nor could he see anything of his route.

The powerful car accelerated now, taking short cuts through the estate until it was in the open country. The men did not speak and Jim began to grow frightened. What did they want? Who were they? Where were they taking him?

Once out of the town, the Jaguar's speed rose to a steady seventy, overtaking other vehicles with an easy grace and Jim found himself reluctantly admiring the driving skill of this frightening person at the wheel.

"This'll do, Bill."

The car slowed down. Jim rose to look out and no one prevented him. On their right was a dutch barn, half full of baled hay, and the Jaguar turned into the farm track at this point.

"Out," snapped the man with the gun.

"Why?"

"Because I said so."

Jim didn't move, but the gun was thudded into his ribs, and the man said, "You'll die if you don't, mister. One more killing means nothing to us."

"Oh, God!"

"That's better. Now. Out of this car and into that barn."

The man called Bill was already striding towards the barn, and Jim decided to take a chance.

He swung his fist at his captor; he tried desperately, in the confined space of the car, to attack his assailant, but the man merely laughed and blocked the blow.

"Doesn't work, mister. Not in a car.

But a gun does work. Now, get out," and the pistol waved in front of his face, with the safety-catch off.

Jim obeyed.

He climbed out, hands shaking with fear, and the man came with him. Bill had vanished into the barn, and Jim walked towards it, with his captor in close attendance.

The man had Jim's briefcase and agency collection-book with him.

"This way."

Jim stepped forward and he was escorted into the barn, warm and dry with the bales forming thick walls, hiding him and his captors from the roads and from prying eyes.

Bill was waiting, standing legs apart and arms folded. He was deep within the barn, and the other man nudged Jim.

"Over near Bill."

"What are you going to do?"

"Ask questions."

"But why . . . why pick on me. . . ?"

The man didn't reply. Instead, he carefully put the briefcase and collecting-book on the floor.

"Your property," he said. "Note that we haven't taken it away. Now," he addressed Jim, "who were you phoning?"

And with startling suddenness, Jim was seized from behind. His arms were locked behind his back, leaving his stomach, chest and face exposed.

Jim struggled; it was no good. Bill had him helpless, pressing strongly on his arms.

"I've got him, George."

"Good. Now we can start in earnest. Your name is James Kennedy and you live at 47 Iburndale Terrace, Crafton. You see, I haven't forgotten. You are a young man, so at that address you will have a pretty young wife, and possibly a family. Or maybe you will have a mother and a father, or it might be lodgings. It's matterless to us. The fact is that you have people at that address. Either you tell us why you are interested in our car, or they will get hurt."

"I'm not interested in your car!"

George leapt forward and plunged his fist twice into Jim's exposed stomach; twice with astonishing speed and paralyzing strength. Jim gasped; the pain grabbed at his innards and he doubled up. But only his head flopped forward; nothing else could move because Bill held him so firmly.

"Why are you interested in our car?"

Jim tried to speak, tried to answer something, but no speech would come. The blow had taken away his breath, his speech.

Again those fists; once, twice. Rapid and pulverizing. Into his stomach, draining away his breath and his strength.

George spoke again, softly and menacingly. "We saw you nosing around it; we saw you look at that house. We are not stupid; you were looking for something. You went to that kiosk and you rang. You said to your friends that you were outside No. 28, and you mentioned our car. The blue Jaguar, you said. Those boxes aren't fully soundproof."

Jim was trying to speak; trying to answer them.

"Let him get his breath back," advised Bill, still clinging to Jim's arms, and George waited, impassive and cruel.

Jim gulped in huge mouthfuls of air, whilst tears of pain ran down his cheeks.

"Well?" said George at length.

Jim still didn't speak; he was thinking of the consequences for Henry Simmons.

George continued. "We have your address, mister. If you don't answer us, we will beat you senseless. Then we'll go to your house. And when you get home —if you get home—we will start on you all over again. We will beat an answer from you."

Jim was sobbing with anxiety, and George said, "Well?"

"I don't know . . . I don't know . . ." he cried.

Again and again those fists pounded into his belly, pummelling, burning, bruising. One after the other, strong and merciless.

Bill relaxed his hold and Jim Kennedy

collapsed into a heap at their feet, grasping his pained and bruised stomach, sobbing with the sheer agony of it. They grabbed his collar and hauled him back to his feet again. George took over from Bill. George now held him, weak and pitiful. They had changed positions.

"When you're ready, Bill," said George and Bill spat on his hands.

Jim tried to shake his head.

"Hold it," said George. "I think he's changed his mind."

They waited, not speaking, as Jim regained his breath. It took a long time, and he stood in a bowed and pained position, held upright by the powerful George.

"Well?"

Jim looked at George and said, "Bastards!"

"Are you going to speak? We have all day; we can reach your house long before you. Wife is it? Young and pretty? She'd look horrible with a razor scar down her lovely face, wouldn't she?"

"No!"

"We've done it before—only once. All our other customers have been more co-operative, mister. Now, I'll ask you once more. Why were you watching our car?"

"That accident . . ."

"Accident?" George looked puzzled.

"Monday night . . . cyclist. . . ."

Bill spoke. "I said he'd been knocked off his bloody bike, George!"

"Shut up!" snarled George. "Go on, mister. What about the accident."

"My friend . . . knocked a man off his bike . . . saw you drive off in the Jaguar and got your number . . . told me . . . I happened to see your car . . . I was ringing him . . ."

"The police!" hissed Bill. "The police. Did the police come to the accident?"

"Yes . . . the man died."

"Died! Good God! Your friend—did he give our number to the police?"

Jim hesitated . . . he realized he knew more than they did . . . they might be frightened away . . .

"Did he?" screeched Bill. "Did he give our number to the cops?"

"I don't know . . . I don't know. . . ."

"Then why give it to you?"

"It's a long story. . . ."

"Who is this friend of yours?"

Jim didn't speak.

"He's being awkward again, Bill."

And without a moment's hesitation Bill launched a further furious attack upon the immobile Jim Kennedy, his powerful fists beating his chest, his face, his stomach. Eyes and mouth, pained and swelling.

And as suddenly, they stopped.

"Your friend's name, mister," demanded George. "We want to speak to him."

Jim's lips were swollen.

"You'll do the same. . . ."

"Not to him. I want to know what he told the police."

"Promise?" the word was difficult to say.

"Promise," repeated George without any feeling.

"Henry Simmons. He lives in a cottage at Drydale. He's an insurance man."

"Right. Now, you haven't seen us. You

haven't seen the car. You were beaten up by two assailants for the money you carried. All right? If any word of this reaches the police, we'll come round to your house."

"You bastards . . . you callous swine. . . ."

George still held him.

Bill said, "And this is to show you that we mean business."

And he thereupon attacked his defenceless victim unmercifully, battering him into near insensibility; and when Bill was tired, they changed places.

Twenty minutes later, the Jaguar left Jim Kennedy senseless on the earthen floor of the dutch barn, lonely, deserted.

He was barely alive.

"Jim? You there?"

Charlie Barnett tapped the receiver of his telephone, but it was dead.

He called the operator and asked, "I had a call only a second or two ago. We were cut off. Can you trace it?"

"I'm sorry, sir. That's impossible."

"Blast!" and he slammed down his receiver.

Charlie Barnett looked at the note pad in front of him; he'd scribbled No. 28 Almond Grove, Southburn and the words "blue Jaguar".

Then Jim had been cut off.

Had the impetuous young devil got himself into hot water?

Barnett rang Embleton police, and asked for PC Christian. He was out, and the duty sergeant answered.

"Charles Barnett here, sergeant," he announced himself. "I'm ringing about that accident involving the cyclist."

"I'm familiar with it."

"You'll remember the driver—Simmons—mentioned a blue Jaguar near the scene."

"I do," and the sergeant sounded weary.

"I gave a description of it to my men —one of them has just rung me. It's parked outside No. 28 Almond Grove, Southburn."

"Are you sure it's the same vehicle,

sir?" The sergeant spoke in a bored, uninterested voice.

"Not certain. He was cut off, sergeant."

"And he hasn't rung back?"

"No."

"Then I suggest we forget it, Mr. Barnett."

"But it's important—and that dead man. It might lead to his identification!"

"There is nothing to connect him with the car," said the bored voice.

"Is your Superintendent there?" demanded Charles Barnett.

"No."

"An Inspector?"

"No."

"Then I demand that you take some action in the matter, otherwise I shall write to the Home Office."

"Where did you say he saw the Jaguar?" The bored tone persisted, but the sergeant was shaken into activity.

"Outside No. 28 Almond Grove, Southburn," repeated Charlie Barnett.

"I'll have someone sent round—it's not

our division, but I'll pass the message along."

"It is urgent. . . ."

"Why?" demanded the sergeant.

"My friend rang off . . ."

"I don't call that a reason for putting the entire police force into a panic, Mr. Barnett. Just leave it with me and we'll have a man sent to take a look at the house."

And with that, the line went dead.

Barnett next rang Kennedy's house; Mrs. Kennedy answered and said that her husband was not back yet.

Barnett left no message and settled down to his tea. He wouldn't inform Henry Simmons yet—he wanted to hear Kennedy's story first.

Jim Kennedy returned to a pained consciousness after they had gone. He struggled to his feet, hardly able to walk, and made his painful way towards the road.

It was growing dark.

Shortly after six o'clock, a uniformed

policeman on a cycle rode up to Almond Grove, Southburn and dismounted almost opposite No. 28.

He checked the address against a note in his pocket book, leaned the cycle against the kerb, then strode up the drive towards the front door.

It was PC Jackson of the local police force, a young man recently out of Training School; consequently, he was alert and keen, with his sights set on a career in the CID.

Before setting out on this enquiry, he'd had the sense to check with the voters' lists for the locality in an effort to establish the name of the occupier of No. 28. He therefore knew the name of the man he was expecting to interview.

He rang the bell.

It was almost dark now; the late winter daylight was losing its fight with the dusk, and as the sound of the bell died away in the hall, a light came on.

Then the door opened.

"Mr. Bourne-Atkins?" asked PC Jackson.

"Yes?" and the question in his voice was easy to hear.

"Er, I have an enquiry, sir. Rather an unusual one."

"Then you must come in," and Bourne-Atkins stepped back to allow his visitor to enter; PC Jackson removed his cap and was shown into the expensively fitted lounge.

"Sit down, constable," said his host. "Sherry?"

"No, thank you. Not on duty. Now, sir. This is briefly the story . . ." and PC Jackson related the history of the road accident involving Mr. Henry Simmons, and he gave due prominence to the presence of the blue Jaguar.

"The situation is this, sir," he continued at length. "We have reason to believe that this car, with two men accompanying it, paid a visit to your house shortly after four o'clock this afternoon."

"A blue Jaguar? I've been at home all afternoon," said Bourne-Atkins, "and

I've had no visitors at all. I can assure you of that."

"Are you absolutely certain?"

"Positive. I don't know anyone with a blue Jaguar car. You must be mistaken."

6

PC JACKSON reported back to his Sergeant in the tiny Sectional office at Southburn.

"Funny, Sergeant. Bourne-Atkins says he had no callers."

"Who says he had?"

"Embleton Police said an insurance agent called Barnett rang them—one of his chaps had seen that car outside this house."

"Did he say which agent?"

"No, he didn't, but it's very strange—you know that young insurance agent with the pretty wife—the one who tried to flog you a life policy?"

"Young Kennedy? He actually succeeded in flogging me one!"

"That's him! Well, his car was parked just up the road from Bourne-Atkins' house—without any lights on. The doors weren't locked. I switched his lights on for him."

"He could be the man who reported it. Did you look for him?"

"I asked around. His car's been there over two hours, Sergeant, but no one's seen Kennedy. Seems odd to me."

"Does it?"

"Well, no one's seen him."

"Know where he lives?"

"Somewhere in Iburndale Terrace."

"That's it. His full address will be in the phone book. Go and find out what's going on, will you? Might be nothing, of course, but Bourne-Atkins has been acting a bit strange lately—well, strange for a retired businessman, anyway."

"Strange? How, Sergeant?"

"Hard to put a finger on—he's been seen talking to some shady characters. Then he vanished, you know. For five days. We didn't make a fuss about it because no one reported him officially missing. But no one knows where he went."

"I'll go and see Kennedy now."

And after learning the precise address, PC Jackson left the office.

Mrs. Kennedy answered the door with a baby in her arms, and Jackson said, "Is your husband in, Mrs. Kennedy?"

"No, I'm afraid not. He should have been back some time ago, but he's often late home."

"Any idea where he is?"

"Somewhere in the district—it's his canvassing day. Is something wrong?"

"No," said Jackson, not wanting to alarm her. "I understand he rang some information to one of our offices today—about a car which was involved in an accident. I just wanted a word with him about it. Perhaps he'd give me a ring when he comes in?"

"I'll tell him," she replied.

PC Jackson excused himself, and left Iburndale Terrace in a thoughtful mood.

So the Sergeant thought Bourne-Atkins was up to something. Had Kennedy, therefore, stumbled upon something important?

PC Keith Jackson decided to delve

deeper into this; first, though, he must ring Embleton Police with his negative report. All he could say was that the occupier of No. 28 denied having any visitors and said he knew nothing about a blue Jaguar car. That was all Jackson could say, although he didn't for one minute believe it was the truth.

The result of Jackson's enquiry was telephoned to the duty Sergeant at Embleton, some twenty five miles away, and, in turn, the duty Sergeant at Embleton rang Charles Barnett with the news.

Barnett listened with dismay; funny he'd not heard from Jim Kennedy himself. It was well over two hours since he'd telephoned that unfinished message.

Barnett decided to ring him again— perhaps his wife had forgotten to deliver his message.

But Mrs. Kennedy answered the telephone. Barnett asked, "Is he back yet, Mrs. Kennedy?"

"No, he isn't Mr. Barnett. I'm getting worried—he's not usually as late as this."

"I wonder where he is?" muttered Barnett, almost to himself.

"A policeman's been to see him," put in Mrs. Kennedy.

"A policeman? What about?"

She explained the reason for PC Jackson's visit and Barnett then told her the full story; he told her about the accident and Jim's part in seeing the car.

"Oh, no!" she cried. "You don't think he's been harmed!"

"No. He's probably watching them or something." Charlie Barnett tried to sound cheerful, but his attempt wasn't very convincing; play-acting over the telephone was almost impossible and Mrs. Kennedy rang off, by now a very worried girl.

What should she do next?

What could she do?

Then her telephone rang again.

Jim!

She hurried to it, praying that it was him; praying he was ringing to say where he was.

"Mrs. Kennedy," she answered quickly.

"This is Middlesbrough General Hospital—duty sister speaking," came the response. "Is that Mrs. June Kennedy?"

"My husband!" she cried. "You've got him there?"

"It's all right, Mrs. Kennedy. Nothing to worry about, so please listen. He is here, in our casualty unit, but he's all right. I'm ringing to let you know."

"But . . . why? What's happened?"

"We don't know. He's been terribly beaten up, Mrs. Kennedy. He was found in the country by a gentleman who was driving into town; the gentleman brought him straight here. He will be allowed home tomorrow."

"Can I see him?"

"I wouldn't advise it, Mrs. Kennedy. He's sleeping now—we have given him something to make him sleep. It will be as beneficial to him as anything else."

"Did he say anything? Why it happened, I mean?"

"Nothing."

"Have you told the police?"

"No. We haven't. Our instructions are not to inform the police unless expressly directed by the patient himself or by his relatives."

"Thank you, sister," said June Kennedy. "May I ring again later tonight?"

"By all means."

June replaced the receiver. She walked back into the living-room with her mind in a turmoil. Beaten up! Her Jim. Why? The police had called, asking for him. Something to do with an accident.

PC Jackson! That was the policeman's name.

She would ring him—he'd been wanting to speak to Jim.

She almost ran back to the telephone to dial the local police station number.

"Southburn Police. PC Jackson speaking."

"It's June Kennedy," she said. "You called a short time ago."

"Yes, Mrs. Kennedy, what's bothering you?"

"It's my husband—he's in Middlesbrough Hospital."

"In hospital!" he cried. "What's the matter with him?"

"He's been beaten up," she explained. "The duty sister rang me—he was found somewhere in the country."

"Where exactly?"

"I don't know. I don't know."

"When was he taken there?"

"I don't know that either . . . I don't know . . ."

"All right. Look, I'll ring the hospital —Middlesbrough General, I presume?"

"Yes."

"I'll ring them, and find out what I can. I'll call you back."

"Thank you," said June Kennedy gratefully, and then she rang Charlie Barnett.

After hearing June Kennedy's story, Charlie Barnett rang Embleton Police.

"The position is this," he bellowed into

the telephone. "I telephoned your duty sergeant nearly three hours ago. I told him that one of my men had reported seeing that blue Jaguar, and that I wanted urgent action because my man's call had been cut off. Now I'm told he is in Middlesbrough General Hospital after being beaten up. I demand some action, Superintendent. This is no way to run a bloody police force. I'm going to write to my MP about this!"

"I will make a full enquiry, sir."

"You're bloody right, you will, Superintendent. I'll see that you do. Where is Kennedy's car? Who assaulted him and why? Why didn't your Sergeant pull his finger out and do something when I rang him?"

"I can't hope to answer those questions without making my own enquiries, Mr. Barnett. I will inform you in due course of the result of my investigations."

"You'd better!" and Charlie Barnett slammed down the telephone.

"Sergeant Tate!" bawled Superintendent Harris, into his intercom, "Come here and bring the message pad with you!"

Meanwhile, in Drydale village, the Simmons family were settling down for the evening.

"How are you feeling, darling?" asked Margaret Simmons.

Henry smiled up at his wife. "Fine," he said. "I had a good day today—did a bit of business, and had time to think about the accident."

"I thought you'd be trying to forget it."

"I should, but I tried to go over it in my mind—to try and decide for myself whether I was at fault."

"And were you?"

"I certainly had more to drink than I should."

"Henry! You mustn't think like that. The cyclist was in the middle of the road. You said he was."

"But I should have been driving so that I could pull up in time."

"Henry. That is a shocking corner and he had no lights on. You said he was wearing a dark coat and he was in the middle of the road; on top of that, it was pouring down. Henry, you didn't stand a chance."

She settled on the sofa at his side, and he leaned forward and kissed her. "At least," he said, "that spot of exercise today has done me a power of good. Anyone ring while I was out? Police or Charlie Barnett?"

"No," she said. "No one at all."

"Obviously nothing's happened then. I shouldn't think they'll find the Jaguar, Margaret. It's a chance in a million, really."

"The police can do a lot—and don't forget, all the other insurance agents are looking out for it!"

"But even if they find it, the driver might not help—he'll deny seeing anything. If he wanted to give evidence for me, he wouldn't have driven away."

"But at least he must be asked."

Then their telephone rang. "I'll get it," Margaret said. "You've finished for the day."

She went into the hall and he heard her say, "Oh, yes, Mr. Barnett. He's here. Yes, fine thank you. No, he's been at work—collecting over at Renwick."

He went through and she handed the telephone to him. "Mr. Barnett," she announced as he took the handset.

"Simmons here."

"Ah, Henry. How's things? I hear you've been at work."

"Best thing to do, I felt."

"Maybe you're right. Now, listen, Henry. You know young Jim Kennedy from Southburn!"

"Young chap—keen type. Met him at a District Conference."

"Yes, well, he spotted your blue Jaguar. Outside a house in Southburn—28 Almond Grove, in fact. Retired businessman's home—chap by the name of Bourne-Atkins."

"Was it his car?"

"No. But listen. Kennedy rang me from a kiosk nearly opposite that house. He was cut off in the middle of his call and now he's been found beaten up, somewhere in the country near Tees-side."

"Good God!" breathed Henry. "Why?"

"We don't know. I rang Embleton Police as soon as Jim was cut off, but they did nothing. The swine! I've told the Superintendent what I think of his men and their lethargy!"

"But . . . why? Why beat Kennedy up?"

"Because he found that Jaguar, I should think. Because he recognized it. Now, I'm ringing you because I'm worried, Henry. I don't know what's going on, and I don't know what young Kennedy has told his attackers."

"But are you sure he was attacked because of that car?"

"We can't be absolutely positive, but what else is there?"

"No idea. What's happening now? You've told the police?"

"Mrs. Kennedy rang her local bobby—he's finding out what happened. Kennedy knew about your accident, of course, so it looks as though you've stirred up a right hornet's nest, Henry Simmons."

"I have, haven't I?"

"Right on your Star Man year too, God help us!"

"I got some new business today—just to keep my hand in."

"Good, but I'm not ringing about business, Henry. I'm ringing to warn you."

"Warn me? Why, for heaven's sake?"

"In case the men in the blue Jaguar decide to pay you a visit."

"Me? They don't even know me, Mr. Barnett! Besides, why would they want to call here?"

"Henry! You must be bloody stupid! They've beaten up young Jim; the chances are he's told them all about you and your accident, which means they must know all about you. If they've beaten him up, it's to stop him talking to the police. That, in turn, means they don't want to be identified. And you saw their car, too—remember?"

"But how do we know it's the same car?"

"We don't *know*, Henry, but it's a bloody fair bet now. Look, cut out the cackle and be on your guard. That's all."

"Sure, we'll be careful. How is Jim, by the way?"

"Dunno. Mrs. Kennedy said he was coming out of hospital tomorrow. I'll try to get over to see him. I want to find out exactly what happened."

"Give him my regards."

"Will do."

"Have they identified the cyclist yet?" asked Henry.

"Don't think so. I'm going to chase the police about that, too. It's possible he's mixed up in the affair as well."

"Be careful," said Henry, without thinking.

"It's you who should be careful, Henry Simmons. 'Bye."

"Cheerio."

Henry replaced his telephone thoughtfully, and then rejoined Margaret and told her the story.

She listened carefuly, her legs curled up on the settee but she didn't smile. Instead, she wore a worried frown, and turned her head to look earnestly at him.

"Henry. You have told me everything, haven't you?"

"Everything? Of course I have! Why? What do you mean?"

"You're not in some other trouble, are you?"

"Trouble? I don't understand."

"I don't know, darling . . . it's just that everything seems so unreal. I mean, Jim Kennedy getting beaten up . . . you knocking down an unknown cyclist . . . it's all mystery and violence . . . it's not like a normal accident."

He moved closer to her. "Darling. I'm not mixed up in anything, if that's what you're thinking. Please believe me. I just don't know what's going on."

She didn't answer; instead she settled down to a book, but her pretty face still bore a look of deep concern.

Henry couldn't fail to notice it. She

couldn't think he was involved in something shady, too! Surely not!

He picked up his briefcase and removed one of his books—there was a bit
of clerical work to do before bedtime—
but his mind wasn't on his task.

He was worried about Margaret. Surely
she didn't believe he was involved in
something crooked?

Then the doorbell.

"For heaven's sake!" cried Margaret.
"They'll wake the children!"

"Coming!" shouted Henry.

It rang again as he hurried to answer
the door, and this time it was
accompanied by loud knocking. Margaret
was also on her feet, looking towards the
door.

Henry switched on the outside light
and opened the door.

Two men stood on the step.

And outside, in the light of the pub
across the road, stood the blue Jaguar.

7

AS the door opened, both men pushed their way into the cottage. "Hey! What's the idea?" cried Henry Simmons.

"Shut up and close the door," snapped the shorter of the two, and both strode menacingly into the living-room.

"This is a private house," cried Henry, going in after them, and he found Margaret standing near the kitchen door, hands to her mouth as if to stifle a scream.

"Shut up and listen!" The smaller one spoke again. "This your missus?"

"Yes, and if you lay a hand—"

"Belt up, mister!" scorned the taller intruder, "and listen to what my mate has to say."

Henry was quiet; he had one eye on Margaret, who stood pale-faced and terrified.

"Are you Simmons?"

"Yes."

"You killed that chap on the bike?"

"He was in the middle—"

"So you knocked him down. Right? You saw a car driving off."

"A blue Jaguar."

"And you told the cops about it."

"I told them that a blue Jaguar with a green mudguard had driven out of the gateway—"

"Why tell them that?"

"The bike had no lights. I might be taken to court for causing death by dangerous driving; if I'm convicted I could lose my licence and that means losing my job. I thought the people in that car might have seen the bike and I thought they would give evidence for me."

"The cops? You gave them the car number?"

"No. I didn't see it."

"You're a liar!" and the tall one brought the flat of his hand hard across Henry's face.

"Henry!"

Henry rubbed his cheek and said, "I couldn't see the number; it was dark and wet."

"I told you we'd panicked!" said the taller man. "You're too hasty, Bill— you've got us into a right bloody mess now."

"Belt up, George! You're a bloody idiot! Think I believe this snivelling twerp? He's told the cops—otherwise how did that little insurance man find us, if he didn't know the number?"

Henry spoke, "I'm an insurance agent myself—my boss gave all our men a description of the car I'd seen. They were all looking for it, but we didn't know its number."

"Why look for it then?"

"I told you why! To ask the driver to give evidence for me in court—to say whether the bike had lights on or not."

"It hadn't," said George. "I can tell you that, but you won't get me or my mate into any bloody courtroom. Now, listen, Simmons—and Mrs. Simmons.

Forget all about the blue Jaguar. Forget you ever saw it."

"But my licence . . . my job . . . my family!"

"Family?" and with the speed of light, the one called Bill moved across the room and seized Margaret by her hair.

She cried out with alarm and pain; Henry moved towards her, but the tall one, George, held up a threatening hand.

"I wouldn't if I were you, Simmons!"

Bill delved into his jacket pocket and dragged out a black handled cut-throat razor; he flicked it sharply and the blade swung from its casing, glistening in the light of the room.

He held it close to Margaret's cheek; very close, and he moved it up and down, smoothly and dangerously.

"Pretty wife you've got, Simmons. Very pretty."

"If you lay one hand on her . . ."

"What will you do? What can you do? You can't do anything, so don't be a nut. You listen to me. You haven't seen us, or our car. If the police find us—and I don't think they will now—you will withdraw your statement. That's all. If you persist in trying to get us to court, your wife's pretty face will be slit open. Your house will be torn apart and if that doesn't stop you, we'll take a look upstairs at the kids."

"But you can't do this . . . you can't!"

"We can, Simmons. We can and we will."

"But why? Why won't you appear?"

"That is our affair and I advise you and your insurance friends to lay off. If we have any more trouble from them, we'll come back here."

"No!" cried Margaret. "No, you can't. . . ."

"In my dictionary, Mrs. Simmons, there is no such word as can't."

"Come on, Bill. They won't talk— they've got too much sense."

Both men made as if to leave the room; the one called Bill pocketed the razor and moved away from Margaret. But as they passed Henry, they seized him, just as they had seized Jim Kennedy.

His arms were whipped tight behind his back, forcing Henry's stomach forward and thereupon George pummelled him with a series of swift, well aimed punches.

And as they beat him, Margaret screamed. When they had finished, Henry fell to the floor, gasping, moaning, trying to be sick, and George said, "That's just an example—a free offering of what we'll do if you disobey us."

And they were gone. The Jaguar roared away as Margaret stooped, crying, over her fallen husband.

"PC Christian," snapped Sergeant Tate, "that fatal accident of yours. Come here and bring the file."

Joe Christian carried the growing file into the Sergeant's office, and stood with it clutched in his hands. The Sergeant seemed to be in one of his moods.

"Got that corpse identified yet?"

"Not yet."

"Then you'd better get something done about it, Christian! There's hell on—I've been hauled before Harris because that insurance chap, Barnett, says we're doing nothing. One of his men got beaten up today after finding a blue Jaguar!"

"Beaten up?"

"In the country—enough to put him in hospital. And now he won't talk—his family's been threatened, so it seems. If he talks, they'll carve his wife and child up."

"The bastards . . ."

"Anyway, there's clearly something bloody funny going on, Christian, and it's your case. Get that blue Jaguar traced, for God's sake!"

Christian turned up the statements in the file. "Light blue, with a damaged wing, painted dull green. Figures 400 in the registration plate."

"Yep. Find that car, Christian. I want to know what's going on."

"We have circulated a description, Sergeant. Every policeman in this district knows about it."

"Forgotten about it, I should think—it takes a nosy insurance man to find it.

Outside a house in Southburn—and the householder denied all knowledge of it. We're watching him now—but it's not his car."

"I'd better go and see Simmons again—he might have remembered something more."

"A good start—and visit Barnett, too. It'll keep him quiet for a bit."

Forty-five minutes later, PC Christian knocked on the door of Hive Cottage, and waited. The lights were on. There was no sound of any television, and yet no one came to the door.

He knocked again, louder.

"They're back!" cried Margaret, clinging to Henry. "They're back, Henry . . ."

"No, darling. No, it's not them. I'm sure . . . they'd have come straight in."

"Don't go . . . please. . . ."

"I must, Margaret. We can't ignore knocks."

"But it's late—nearly nine o'clock."

They listened; they heard the sound of the door knob turning, and Margaret

114

stifled a scream. Henry held her; then a voice.

"Mr. Simmons? You all right? It's PC Christian."

"Oh," he said. "Oh, thank God. . . ."

Then he called, "Come in . . . I'm coming."

He met the policeman in the hall, and Henry found he was still shaking, still nervous.

"You feeling all right?" asked PC Christian, and then he saw Margaret, her eyes red with crying, her handkerchief wrapped tight about her fist.

"Mr. Simmons! Have they been here? Have you been threatened?"

Henry and Margaret looked at each other; their faces gave PC Christian his answer.

"When?" he said, then added, "We've heard about Mr. Kennedy."

Neither of them spoke.

"Look," said PC Christian. "Tell me what happened—I'll promise to help in any way I can. I know they've been, and

I want to know what happened. I'm one of the few people who can help."

"But they said if I told the police. . . ."

"They'd come back?"

"Yes."

"OK. Then tell me as a private individual. I'll honour your wishes."

Margaret looked at them both, terror showing in her eyes, now appearing dark against her pale skin.

"Tell him, Henry."

"They came about half-an-hour ago. Came straight in. Threatened my wife with a cut-throat razor and they gave me a punch or two in the stomach. Said they'd beat us up, and the kids, and the house, if I didn't forget the Jaguar and them."

"The car number? Did you see it this time?"

"No. I didn't. That's God's honest truth, Mr. Christian. And I couldn't describe them if I wanted to. So don't ask me. But you must not look for that car now. I want it forgotten—you must, for my family's sake."

116

"But it means you'll risk losing your licence—you've no witness."

"That's unimportant now. I'd rather lose my licence than have my family roughed up—besides, if you did trace them, they wouldn't help me, would they? It's a sheer waste of time. So forget it. I'll go to court and see what happens."

"It's not you we are concerned about now, is it? What we want to know is what they're up to. Why all this trouble? The reason I came was to see if you could remember anything else about the incident—anything, however insignificant it may appear to you."

"You know what my answer is to that one, don't you?"

PC Christian sighed, "I can't compel you to give answers, and I appreciate your reasons."

"There was nothing else. That's the truth."

"I believe you. You know about Mr. Kennedy?"

"Yes, Barnett rang."

"He's badly beaten up and he won't

talk either. His family will be injured if he talks."

"He found their car," commented Henry.

"I suspect he got its registration number—if so, he's the only man who knows it. And he won't tell us. God knows what they're up to. Anyway, I won't bother you any more. I'll have our chaps keep a discreet watch on your house. Keep your doors locked at night, and don't let strangers in. Don't be afraid to ring us up if there is any further trouble, will you? Now, I'm going to see your Mr. Barnett on the way home. Want me to tell him about your visitors?"

"Please," said Henry. "He's the one who's pushing things. Tell him to lay off, will you? Or else someone's going to get seriously hurt."

"I'll tell him. I'll let myself out," and PC Christian left them to their misery.

"Don't leave me, Henry," pleaded Margaret when they were alone.

PC Jackson, over in Southburn, had

returned from the hospital with little to report. The hospital authorities had reluctantly allowed him to interview Kennedy, but the battered man wouldn't talk; he simply refused to tell the police about his appalling injuries and he'd said he would put his wife and family at risk by talking.

PC Jackson, in spite of his overwhelming desire to get to the bottom of the affair, respected Kennedy's reticence, and promised to inform the night-duty man and ask him to keep an eye on the house overnight.

"What about your car? I saw it in Almond Grove this evening. Want it taking home?"

"Would you mind? I left it unlocked—keys are in my jacket, somewhere in the hospital. I'd be happier if it was at home."

"So would we. It's a standing invitation to thieves as it is. I'll move it for you. Where's your garage?"

"Behind the house. It's got No. 47 painted on the door, like the house."

"Right. Now look, Mr. Kennedy. I

know you've been through a tough time; I know your family has been threatened, but I want to find out what those characters are up to. They've got to be stopped. If you do change your mind. . . ."

Kennedy spoke through cracked lips. "I'll remember you first," was all he said, and so Jackson had left, after getting the keys to Kennedy's Austin.

To PC Jackson's relief, the Austin was still in the position he'd found it earlier.

He climbed in and switched on the interior lights in order to see the position of the switches and dials.

And as he searched, his eagle eyes spotted the notebook lying on the shelf beneath the dashboard; his detective intuition made him realize that a man like Kennedy, looking for a vehicle, might have made a note about it. Might have made a note about this street, this house.

He flicked open the book.

There was a rough note on the last page —it said, "Accident—Simmons. Blue Jag: 400. Green front wing."

And there, underneath, was an arrow

pointed to the Registration number PDF40Q.

"Great!" beamed PC Jackson. "Great! I've got the bastards now!"

8

PC JACKSON drove the Austin round to Iburndale Terrace and told Mrs. Kennedy that he would garage the vehicle for her; she asked after her husband and Jackson assured her that he was fit and well and merely resting.

He said nothing about the Jaguar, nor the notebook in the car, but simply put the car away, dropped the latch on the garage door and returned to the station. He experienced a new eagerness to get to the bottom of the mystery.

But tonight, there was little he could do. In order to check the owner of that car, he must contact its local registration authority, but all such offices were closed.

He could, however, ring the local police and ask them to treat the enquiry as an emergency; they might go round to the Taxation Offices themselves and look up the name of the registered owner of the blue Jaguar. It seemed a feasible thing to do; its owners were clearly criminals, up to no good and dishing out violence with carefree abandon.

He strode into the little brick-built office and his Sergeant, by the name of Bailey, listened to his story.

"Told anyone, lad?"

"CID. One of them is watching the house in Almond Grove."

"Queer set up. Right. Try to trace that Jaguar—get the local police to trace it for you."

Jackson began what was for him a routine task. PDF40Q was one of the series issued in Gloucester; he therefore rang Gloucestershire Constabulary and asked for the usual enquiries to be made.

Gloucestershire Police said they would ring back as soon as possible, and PC Jackson settled down to write out a draft report, giving details of his progress to date.

He settled at the office typewriter and saw himself heading into the ranks of the Criminal Investigation Department. What had been a rather mundane and routine enquiry was developing into something exciting and adventurous.

He was discovering something of real concern to his own beat—to this section; it now had little bearing on that fatal accident over in Embleton Division.

Jackson saw himself winning a commendation from his Chief Constable; that sort of recognition was the first step towards CID work.

At Embleton Police Station, however, things had cooled off. PC Christian returned after his talks with Henry Simmons and Charles Barnett, and now felt concerned for these people. As he had done yesterday, he was now working overtime—the money would be handy.

Clearly, the dead man had been involved in some illegal activity and his death had started a chain reaction which was rapidly spreading to innocent people.

So far as PC Christian was aware, no one knew the number of the Jaguar; no one knew the identity of the dead cyclist.

Then, over and above this, the fate of Henry Simmons lay in the balance. He'd been right, of course. Even if they did trace the owners of the Jaguar, they would never give evidence for Simmons in court—not men like that. They would simply deny being near the scene.

From Simmons' point of view, therefore, it was a waste of time trying to find that car, but from the criminal aspect, it was vital that the men were identified.

Christian must rely on the observation of his pals and colleagues all over the country who, he hoped, would read the circulated particulars and stop the car.

That young insurance man at Southburn had seen it; but they'd frightened him into silence.

Then the office telephone rang.

"Embleton Police. PC Christian speaking."

"Fingerprints, Scotland Yard," came the faint response.

"Yes," shouted PC. Christian. "What can we do for you?"

"We got a set of prints from you this

afternoon—sent down on the train, and marked urgent—fatal accident—you know about it?"

"I'm dealing with it. Any luck?"

"Yes. We've got the prints on file, Mr. Christian. Your dead man has quite a record."

"Has he? Who is he?"

"Paul Francis Edmunds. He's thirty-four years old, and has done time on a few occasions. He was released from Wakefield Gaol two months ago."

"Address?"

"He hasn't one. No fixed abode. Until his last stretch in prison he lodged in Birmingham—worked for a light industrial firm. Good worker when he put his mind to it."

"What sort of convictions has he then?"

"Robbery mainly. Robbery with violence; armed robbery, assault; handling stolen goods, burglary and taking motor vehicles without the owner's consent. Did a three year stretch for handling—that was his last one."

"That's very interesting."

"We'll confirm in writing, of course, and we'll send a copy of his criminal record for you. Photograph and antecedents will be included. Was he involved in something in your area?"

"Dunno," said Joe Christian. "Got himself killed when riding a bike without lights. Ironic, isn't it?"

"I see what you mean. OK. Anything else?"

"No. His name will do. Thanks."

"Cheerio."

And the caller rang off; doubtless it was a detective working late turn at the Yard's fingerprint records department, but at least his search of the records had given a name to Joe Christian's corpse.

The inquest could be opened, perhaps tomorrow; evidence of identification would have to come from the Yard's photograph of the deceased but Joe felt it would be acceptable to the coroner. It would have to be—there was nothing else for the moment.

What about relatives? Edmunds must

surely have some relatives—sisters, brothers, parents? Maybe he was married?

He should have asked, but such details would be in the fellow's antecedent history; it would have to wait until copies arrived. But they would take time to arrive at Embleton.

Had Edmunds been riding without lights at the time of the accident? Only one man could tell the court the truth—Henry Simmons. And if he lied, no one would know.

Somehow, Joe Christian believed in Henry Simmons.

With a sigh, he wrote the message in the Occurrence Book, and then typed a transcript for the file about the fatal accident.

Now the proceedings could start. Henry Simmons must be summoned to appear at Embleton Magistrates' Court in due course. Whether the charge was one of careless driving, dangerous driving or possibly causing death by dangerous driving was yet to be decided. That decision rested upon Superintendent Harris.

At nine o'clock the following morning, Wednesday, Superintendent Harris strode into his office, and the Divisional Clerk hurried in after him, carrying the Occurrence Book. Hard on the heels of the Sergeant was the duty Inspector who would have to answer any queries put by the Superintendent.

"Ah!" beamed Harris when he read the account of the telephone call from Fingerprints. "Got that body identified, eh? Edmunds. Convicted too. Have we found that Jaguar yet, Inspector?"

"No, sir. But Southburn police say it's been seen in their area. The man who saw it has been attacked and is in hospital. He won't talk now—he's been beaten up; someone's scared the living daylights out of him."

"Have they? Where was it seen?"

The Inspector told his boss about the house and the retired businessman; then he gave a brief account of Henry Simmons' visitors last night.

"Hrrumph," grunted Harris. "Nasty specimens, by the look of things. Wonder what the dead man was up to that night? What have Southburn done about that house? What do they know about its occupant?"

"Mr. James Bourne-Atkins, sir. They are watching him."

"That all?"

"They did interview him, sir. He denied all knowledge of the car or its occupants."

"Then he's obviously mixed up in the affair. I think this is a job for the Crime Squad, Inspector."

"Couldn't our local CID cope, sir?"

"Could do, but it looks as though something bigger is involved. I'll ring Headquarters and tell Detective Superintendent MacCready what we know. I'm sure it's a job for his lads."

"There is one problem, sir."

"Is there?"

"Henry Simmons and that man

Kennedy from Southburn. Both their families have been threatened if we take further action."

"I realize that, but we can't let those hoodlums dictate to us, Inspector. Give the families protection—I'll organize something at the Southburn end. We're going after those people, Inspector, and I'm going to suggest someone has a strong word with Bourne-Atkins, too. Doesn't know about the Jaguar! Does he think we believe that? He must think we're all fools!"

"Yes, sir," and the Inspector left as Harris picked up his telephone and rang Headquarters CID.

At about the time Superintendent Harris was telephoning Detective Superintendent MacCready, Jim Kennedy was walking painfully out of Middlesbrough General Hospital. His eyes and lips were discoloured and swollen and his entire body seemed to ache; every movement was a separate agony, but his night in hospital had given him a much needed rest. His brain was alert.

They had dosed him so that he slept fitfully and they had attended to his wounds with compassion and skill; apart from the pain, and the feeling that he looked like a battered boxer, he felt surprisingly fit.

But Jim Kennedy had learned his lesson. No more would he interfere with the business of others; no more would he poke his nose into affairs which were of no concern to him.

He had laid his family open to violence of a type he had never before encountered, and it was all for something which had nothing to do with him at all. Certainly, he felt sorry for Henry Simmons.

But Henry Simmons must have been driving fast, or carelessly, or unreasonably, otherwise he wouldn't have knocked the cyclist down.

A taxi was waiting for Kennedy at the hospital entrance and within minutes he was on his way home.

He would take a week off work; he wasn't competing for the company's Star Man award.

Not this year, anyway.

Also at about this time, PC Jackson was looking down at the message pad in Southburn Police office.

Gloucestershire had telephoned back at three o'clock this morning in response to his query about the Jaguar, and they had left a message with the night duty man.

"PDF40Q," the message read. "This belongs to a Morris 1100, at present in Stroud. Owner been seen—car still there. No similar number issued to a Jaguar. Sorry."

"False number! A bloody false number!" cried PC Jackson. "That's done it."

So he was no further forward. The Jaguar was carrying a set of false number-plates. So who was the owner? What was its correct number?

Jackson felt dismayed—so far, everything had gone his way. All that remained was the identification of the two men in the Jaguar. And now that chance had slipped from his grasp.

The only answer was to find that Jaguar again, and that was like looking for a needle in a haystack.

Or he could have another chat with Mr. Bourne-Atkins.

He was the only identifiable link in the chain, and Jackson was convinced he knew something. PC Colin Jackson, therefore, collected his cap and decided to walk to Almond Grove. He scribbled a note to the Sergeant giving his whereabouts.

Next, he switched the telephone through to the Sergeant's house and let himself out, dropping the latch as he went.

En route, PC Jackson worked out his plan of action. He would give no hint that he was suspicious of Bourne-Atkins; that would clearly be the wrong approach.

Instead he must continue in the vein of that initial interview; he would conduct his questioning as if he had received confirmation that the Jaguar had been seen parked outside No. 28, and that two men had been seen entering the house.

And PC Jackson would persist until he learned something.

For him, a satisfactory conclusion to this case could mould his entire future, and he had no intention of letting it slide from his grasp. He knew that senior officers were showing more than a passing interest in the events of late, and last night his Sergeant had dropped a strong hint that the Superintendent wanted the Crime Squad calling in.

His own Superintendent was going to discuss the matter with Superintendent Harris of Embleton today—and Jackson knew what that meant.

It meant the case would be taken from him, and it would pass into the hands of some high-ranking detective.

But so far, it was still in his hands; the local CID had finished observations on Bourne-Atkins' house on the advice of their Detective Sergeant. People were beginning to notice them.

And so, Colin Jackson strode on his way, enjoying the fresh air and the exercise, and by twenty past nine, he was entering Almond Grove.

His first reaction was to look for the blue Jaguar, but it was nowhere to be seen. Not that he'd really expected it to be there. But there was a car outside the house—a black Wolseley, not unlike those used by Scotland Yard. A beautiful machine, cared for and obviously the pride of its owner. A car maintained like new.

Bourne-Atkins' own, perhaps?

He might be out, of course, but that fact could be elicited later; Jackson was now level with the Wolseley.

He glanced at it, admiring its condition, and began to walk up the garden path.

His knocking on the door was loud, and it quickly resulted in footsteps in the hall; the door opened and Bourne-Atkins stood before him, pale-faced and taut.

"Oh," he said. "It's PC Jackson, isn't it?"

"Yes. I'd like to talk to you again."

"I'm afraid I've got important company, Mr. Jackson. Could you call later?"

Jackson noted the other's nervousness; twice in a matter of seconds, he looked over his shoulder into the house. His tongue continually flickered across his dry lips.

"It is important," continued Jackson, his anxiety to solve the case rising above his courtesy.

"An hour then? Give me an hour?"

Then, from behind Bourne-Atkins there appeared another man, tall and smartly dressed.

"Don't let us interrupt you, Mr. Bourne-Atkins," said the man. "We can wait. You won't be long, officer?"

"No, of course not," responded Colin Jackson.

"Come inside then."

Bourne-Atkins turned back into the house, looking haggard and weary. He led them into the lounge. Jackson followed after closing the front door, and inside he found yet another man, a shade smaller than his colleague.

"Well?" asked Bourne-Atkins, not looking directly at the young policeman.

"I called the other day, Mr. Bourne-Atkins, enquiring about a blue Jaguar."

He nodded. The two men looked at one another, then at the young policeman.

"Well," continued PC Jackson, "we have received further information about it. We have obtained its registration number which has proved false, and we have interviewed other witnesses who swear that it was parked here, and we have a description of the two men . . ."

PC Jackson looked at the two men standing with Bourne-Atkins. They meant nothing to him; they were guests, and yet. . . . Jackson's brain began to work; his words drained away as he gazed earnestly at these men. But his surveillance of them had an alarming effect.

One of them whipped a small snub-nosed pistol from his trousers pocket, levelled it at Jackson and said, "Bourne-Atkins talked . . . don't move. Either of

138

you. George. Help me. We're taking these two away. Bourne-Atkins—you first. Walk ahead of me and get into the Wolseley. Officer—you as well."

9

PC JACKSON whipped round.

"You've got rid of that Jaguar!"

"Move!" screamed the man. "Move. Outside—you as well, Bourne-Atkins."

The taller man came close to PC Jackson and said, "Out. No funny stuff, copper. You're coming for a ride with us. . . ."

"I haven't told him . . . I told him nothing," spluttered Bourne-Atkins. "You must believe me."

"We don't," snapped the shorter man. "Now get moving."

Jackson stood his ground; the man near him hissed, "If you're going to make a hero of yourself, young man, you've chosen the wrong people. If you don't move, you'll get shot. I'm not play-acting, either."

Bourne-Atkins was saying, "Come on,

Mr. Jackson. Please. You don't know these people."

"It's my job to find out all I can," snapped PC Jackson. "Everything. You are all under arrest; I'm now going to ring for assistance."

"You're bloody well not, mate," and the tall man made a grab for the young policeman; but Jackson was young and fleet. He dodged the huge hand, his cap flying off with the movement, turned and delivered a swift, paralysing blow to his assailant's stomach. The man bent forward in agony and as Jackson brought the edge of his hand hard down on the other's neck, his companion stepped forward.

He had the pistol.

"Stop!" he cried, "Stop!"

Jackson looked up; his blow had had its effect and the big man collapsed to the floor. His colleague stepped in.

"Stop!" he shouted, "Stop, for God's sake."

"Try and stop me, bastard," hissed

Jackson, standing like an enraged wrestler. "Just you try to stop me."

"Mr. Jackson . . . please . . ." Bourne-Atkins was burbling in the background. "You mustn't!"

At his feet, the big man was stirring; the other said, "Now, no more of that. Into the car, officer—and you, Bourne-Atkins."

PC Jackson said nothing; he once more stood his ground as the fallen man groaned and moved his hands to his painful neck.

"I repeat. You are all under arrest. I am going to ring for assistance." Jackson spoke slowly, but the man on the floor said, "Kill him, kill the bastard . . ."

"No!" cried Bourne-Atkins. "No. For God's sake. . . ."

The man with the gun spoke, "Into the car. Come along, Jackson, or whatever they call you. If George says kill, he means it. And I've got the gun."

As George gathered himself from the carpet, PC Jackson launched himself at the gunman.

"You're not taking me in that car, mate," snarled Jackson and the gunman reeled back under the sudden, unexpected onslaught; he tripped over the hearth rug and fell to the floor, shouting for George.

Jackson had him; he was lying on top of his victim, one hand around his throat, the other feeling for the gun. Bourne-Atkins stood back, clearly terrified for PC Jackson, but not offering to come to his assistance.

"Get that gun," cried his victim. "Grab it, George!"

George was on his feet now, shaky, but mobile, and he heard the command.

He crossed towards his pal who was helpless now, firmly held down by PC Jackson, but that right hand still clutched the pistol, waving it uselessly in the air. Jackson couldn't seize it—his hands were occupied in keeping the man pinned to the floor.

And as George moved, Bourne-Atkins moved too.

"No," he screeched. "No. You mustn't."

"Belt up, will you?" And with that George levelled a kick at Bourne-Atkins stomach; the older man ducked, but the kick caught him in the groin.

George had got the pistol.

In a lightning movement, he raised it above his head; Jackson knew he must release the little man on the floor beneath him; the man struggled.

But George brought the butt of the pistol hard down on PC Jackson's head. There was a blinding crash, pain, and Colin Jackson crumpled to the floor, unconscious.

"He's a terrier all right," said George, and there was just a hint of pride in his voice. "I like a man who'll put up a fight. Now, Bourne-Atkins. A macintosh. Get a macintosh to cover his uniform—we'll carry him out to the car."

"But. . . ."

"Don't argue, man! Between us—two of us will carry him out; I can guarantee no one will take the slightest bit of notice, and if they do, you will say he's ill . . . a friend who's ill. Right?"

"Do you have to take him?"

"He's too dangerous to ignore."

"But where? What are you going to do with him?"

"We'll worry about that later. My only concern is to get him out of here and stop him passing information to his colleagues. Now, what about that macintosh?"

Detective Superintendent MacCready had listened to Harris and said, "I've got the picture Jack. Right. I'll have the Crime Squad look into it."

Then MacCready had telephoned the Crime Squad offices in Middlesbrough and relayed the information to Detective Inspector Hutchins.

The Crime Squad were a comparatively new innovation, for they belonged to no particular police force. Their members were drawn from neighbouring forces, and were usually based in a suitably convenient office, often within a building used as a Police Headquarters. But their territory ranged throughout the region from which its members were drawn, or it even ranged beyond those boundaries. They were practically freelance detectives.

MacCready had felt this task might be a job for them, for they specialized in travelling criminals; the knowledge possessed by the local CID was often too parochial to be of any real practical use in a major enquiry.

And so Inspector Hutchins had listened.

"Have we any knowledge of any of these characters, sir?"

"Only the dead cyclist, Fred," and he gave brief particulars. "But his record is being sent up from the Yard by train. Should be here later today."

"What about those insurance agents? Think they'll talk?"

"Hard to say. Certainly worth a try, I'd say, but they've both been terrified. Young Kennedy—he's the one over at Southburn—had one hell of a beating up."

"Not to worry, sir. We'll treat 'em like

lambs. Who's looking after the Southburn end of the enquiry?"

"There's a fiery young constable called Jackson who set a hare off at that end. The local CID chap kept observations on Bourne-Atkins' house, but he couldn't stay there all day. Nothing happened when he was there, and he's been withdrawn. Sergeant Bailey at Southburn will fix you up with details."

"Any higher rank there?"

"Nope. It's a sectional station—only carries a sergeant and three constables; one of them is in plain clothes."

"OK sir. We'll get over there, too. Anything known about Bourne-Atkins?"

"Not a great deal. He's a retired businessman who came here three or four years ago. No criminal tendencies as far as we know. Leads a quiet sort of life, by and large."

"Family?"

"Has a son over in Canada; his own wife died three or four years ago. Cancer. Died before he came here."

"Lives alone then?"

"Yes. Nice place. Nothing too pretentious, but of late he's been keeping away from his usual haunts."

"Why?"

"No idea. Told his friends he didn't feel too well—according to them he doesn't look well, either, but he won't have anyone in to look after him. We got whispers—nothing more—the friends got a feeling he is hiding something."

"Mmm," said Inspector Fred Hutchins. "He's obviously mixed up in something, either personal or criminal. Anyway, I'll send our scouts out and we'll ferret something, sir."

"Thanks, Fred. Keep in touch, won't you?"

"Naturally."

Even as they were talking, an early-turn policeman was heading home for his breakfast after patrolling a rural area some ten miles out of Tees-side.

He had been high into the hills of the locality, keeping a watch for cattle trucks which were suspected of stealing sheep from the open moorland strays, but as so often happened, his journey had been fruitless.

And now he was homeward bound; his little station was manned only by himself. He was a country beat constable called Alan Makins, and he was a man who was proud of his job.

He drove steadily homewards, intending to arrive at about nine thirty, which was the time his wife expected him. She'd have eggs and bacon ready and a cup of hot, sweet coffee.

As he drove through Anderton village, the milkman flagged him down.

"Morning, Jack. What's up?" asked PC Makins.

"Nothing really, Mr. Makins, but it's summat at the pub."

"Any ideas?"

"A car. There's a car been left there all night, and it's still there this morning. Doesn't belong to anybody in Anderton, and there's no one staying at the pub."

"Seen it?"

"Yes. Blue Jaguar. Nice car, too. Stan doesn't know whose it is."

Stan was the landlord.

"Blue Jaguar? Hang on, Jack. I think we're looking for one like that."

PC Makins flicked through his notes which dangled on a pad on the dashboard and he found the description.

"Here we are, Jack. Blue Jaguar with a damaged front mudguard; the mudguard's been painted green. Temporary repair job, I'd say."

"That's it, Mr. Makins. This'n's got a green mudguard."

"Right. Thanks. I'll go straight there."

He turned around and drove the three hundred yards to the Black Bull. Parking his police mini-van at the front he strode eagerly around to the rear.

Sure enough, the blue Jaguar was there, alone on the makeshift car-park at the rear.

He looked at it; the front offside mudguard was damaged and had been hastily repaired and repainted with a green undercoat. The registration number was ADO754U

"The one we're looking for has 400 in the number," he said. "Ah well. Could be it, I suppose."

He knocked on the back door of the public house, and Stan Bradshaw answered it.

"Hello, Mr. Makins. Bit early for a visit, isn't it?"

"You're telling me! It's that Jaguar in the car-park I'm interested in, Stan."

"Oh, that. Come in then."

Makins followed the landlord through to the bar where he was getting ready for opening time at ten thirty. Makins was saying, "Jack told me about it. Reckons it doesn't belong to anyone in the village."

"Nope. No one here has got a thing like that."

"Could be a visitor."

"Could be, if we had any in the place. I've got none, and there's none in Anderton just now."

"You sure?"

"Ask around, Mr. Makins. We know what goes on here."

"When did the car arrive then?"

"Sometime last night. We have a bar full of locals—no strangers at all. It wasn't there at six o'clock when we opened, and it was there at half-past ten when we closed. That's all I can say."

"No one saw it come?"

Stan shook his grey head, "Nope. No one saw anything."

"Anyone touched it?"

"Not to my knowledge. Does it matter?"

"I want fingerprints off it, Stan. Our CID chaps will come along to give it a going over. If it has been stolen, there might be prints you see. Help us to find who took it."

"I see. Well, I haven't touched it."

"Good. OK. I'll go and see what I can find out from the office."

"Right. You'll be back?"

"Later. Our CID will be first here, Stan. Big drinkers they are as a rule. You'll do a bit of business this morning!"

"I can do with it."

PC Makins drove home in an excited mood. It wasn't often an event of any significance came his way, and he regarded this as a job which would occupy him for the rest of the day. Immediately he got home, he rang his sectional office.

"Makins, Sergeant. I think I've got an abandoned car on my pitch. That blue Jaguar, you know. Something to do with that fatal accident over near Embleton."

"Where is it, Alan?"

"Behind the Black Bull in Anderton. Description fits, but the registration plate's different."

"What is the number?"

"ADO754U"

"Which registration authority is that? Any idea?"

"Lincolnshire—the Holland area."

"I'll ring Information Room to see if it's been nicked. I'll get the CID out as well. You'll be having breakfast now?"

"Yes. I can smell the bacon and eggs. . . ."

"Enjoy it, and I'll ring you back in

three-quarters of an hour. I'll ring
Embleton too—to see if this is the Jaguar
they're seeking."

"Thanks."

The telephone rang in Hive Cottage,
Drydale, and Margaret Simmons
answered it.

"Mrs. Simmons?"

"It's PC Christian, at Embleton. How
are you now? Have they been back at
all?"

"No. We've not heard anything since
that night, thanks. I'm much better now
—it was all like a bad dream."

"What about your husband? How is
he?"

"Oh, Henry's all right. He's out just
now. He's just gone up to the post
office."

"I wanted a word with him, actually.
How long will he be?"

"Ten minutes or so. I'll ask him to ring
you."

"Please."

"Has any decision been made about the

accident yet?" she asked. "Henry keeps wondering whether he'll have to go to court."

"I don't know, I'm afraid. The file is with our boss at the moment. I'll try and chase things up. I'll let you know the position as soon as possible."

"Thanks."

"Has he got his car back yet?"

"No. He rang the garage this morning —it will be ready this afternoon."

"Good. Make sure he rings me, won't you?"

"I won't forget to tell him."

Henry Simmons returned and was given the message.

"Did he say what it was for?" he asked. "Couldn't he have spoken to you?"

"I didn't ask, Henry. He sounded excited about something."

Henry went through to the telephone and dialled Embleton Police Station, and asked for PC Christian.

"Ah," said Henry as Christian answered the telephone. "You rang me."

"Yes. It's about that blue Jaguar, Mr. Simmons."

"What about it?" Henry tensed at the mention of that car; thoughts of violence tore at his mind and he waited.

"We think we've found it. Behind a village pub, but the number doesn't tally."

"Then surely it will be a different car —mine had a green mudguard."

"So has this one. We'd like you to have a look at it, Mr. Simmons. To identify it for us."

"Hey! Wait a minute!" cried Henry. "You don't expect me to risk my wife and self again, surely? If I confirm that it is the car, they'll be back here and they'll tear the house to pieces. No thank you, Mr. Christian."

Joe Christian sighed.

"It is important, Mr. Simmons. Important from another angle, not necessarily your accident. There's talk of big scale crime."

"Then surely I'd be in more danger than I am now. I'm sorry, Mr. Christian.

I daren't. Call me a coward if you like, but I've a wife and family to consider. As I said when you called, I'll go to court and forget about that car."

"Suppose we drove it past your house? If we rang you in advance to give you an approximate time? You could look out of your window . . . we could telephone you to ask if it was the car in question."

"Would I have to give evidence anywhere?"

"No. All we must do is establish whether this is the car seen by you at the scene of that fatal accident—we want to establish a connection between it and the dead cyclist."

"OK. I'll do that. Drive it past and I'll look out of the window. Make sure none of those men are about."

"Thanks. It might take a day or so—we've got to be sure the car's been abandoned first."

"I appreciate that. By the way, any news of the dead man—his identity, I mean?"

"Yes. I'm sorry—we should have told

you. We learned only yesterday—his name is Paul Francis Edmunds."

"Local?"

"No. No fixed address. He's a criminal, Mr. Simmons. A dangerous, highly skilled criminal."

"I see," whistled Henry Simmons. "I wonder what he was doing there?"

"If we can answer that, we'll be very happy people. Cheerio."

"Bye."

And Henry Simmons replaced his telephone. So that was it. He'd knocked down a criminal, who was probably plotting something.

Now the mystery and the violence had a reason. He decided not to tell Margaret about it.

The beautiful Wolseley car with PC Jackson in the rear seat, was driven carefully through Middlesbrough and branched off into the country.

Jackson was conscious; he saw they'd dressed him in an old raincoat and that his police cap was missing. From outside the car, he looked like an ordinary passenger, but where were they going?

In the front, Bourne-Atkins sat in silence, looking directly ahead, and beside Jackson was the smaller man who nursed a pistol on his lap.

No one spoke.

It must have been nine or ten miles out of the town when the car turned off the main road; it drew slowly round a corner and into a narrow lane. The driver accelerated and the powerful Wolseley picked up speed again.

Jackson tried to get his bearings. He wasn't familiar with this part of the area, and he hadn't been able to read the signposts from this low position in the rear. Each time he leaned forward, the gunman had pressed him back with the barrel of the pistol.

Then a farm. A barn at the roadside. They were turning towards it, along a farm track, dirty and thick with the mud of a damp winter, until the car stopped behind the farmhouse.

Jackson looked out at the scene. Hens

running around the farmyard, scattering noisily ahead of the car, a litter of piglets in a sty and they ran as the car moved into position. A black and white mongrel dog, wagging a welcome. Strands of hay and straw blowing around. An ordinary farm, nearly a mile from the road.

"Out," snapped the gunman, whom Jackson now knew as Bill. He prodded Jackson with the gun and Colin struggled to climb from his cramped position.

He was out; Bill was struggling now, easing himself from the same door which wasn't easy. Jackson noticed this. George was talking to Bourne-Atkins; his attention was diverted.

PC Jackson acted swiftly. He ran as fast as his legs would carry him. He ran for the corner of the farmhouse, intending to turn round it. If he got that far, he could perhaps hide. Or attract attention from the road.

But Bill was out of the car, too. Bill had the pistol.

Jackson heard the shout; the cry to stop. But he ran all the faster, not looking

160

behind. The corner of the building seemed a long way off.

Then a shot rang out.

10

THE shot went wide. Colin Jackson heard its horrifying whine as he instinctively ducked, but the pistol cracked again.

The corner was too far away, then a pain. Piercing, sudden, horrible. In his back. Colin Jackson felt himself pushed forward, as if smacked on the back by a powerful hand. He could see the corner of the house; he wanted to reach the corner of that house. He wanted to turn the corner of the house. But his legs were weak. There was that pain in his back. Biting, crushing his will to continue.

His legs. Weak. Knees had no strength at all. Nothing. . . .

Misty. . . .

The pain. Gasping for breath.

He fell. He fell full length as he ran, his hands breaking the weight of his fall, but he couldn't move any more. God! The pain now . . . in his back, his lungs . . . legs numb.

Running steps nearby. Anxious voices. Bourne-Atkins saying, "You've killed him . . ."

"I'm not dead," he wanted to say. "I'm not dead . . . just give me five minutes. I'll be all right. I'll show those bastards . . . I'll fix 'em for ever . . ." But he was very tired. His eyes closed. So peaceful . . . a cold hand on his face. Strong arms lifting him. God! Be careful. Watch it . . . my back! The pain . . . oh . . . ! Then blackness. Nothing else. Blissful unconsciousness.

Bill stood aside as Bourne-Atkins and George carried the silent figure into the house and laid him on the floor.

"You are bastards. aren't you?" snapped Bourne-Atkins. "Real out-and-out bastards. Shooting a man in the back."

Bill said nothing, but George was examining the still form of PC Colin Jackson.

"You've done it this time, Bill. What now?"

"Let me go," said Bourne-Atkins. "I don't want to get involved in this. . . ."

"You stay right where you are, mister." George almost hissed the words at him. "Not one step out of this place. Not one bloody step."

"But. . . ."

"Shut up."

Bill came closer to the still form of the shot policeman, and stooped down to him.

"Is he. . . ?"

"No. He's alive, Bill. But bad . . . what do we do? A doctor?"

"We can't get a bloody doctor! Don't be so stupid!"

"But he'll die. . . ."

"Better for us if he does, isn't it? Can't talk. He's been the fly in our ointment. . . ."

"Suppose we take him away from here, in the Wolseley, and dial 999. Tell 'em there's a poorly man in a field, or something . . . then clear off. They come and find him; take him to hospital. . . ."

Bill shook his head, "Nope. If he

164

survives, he'll talk. He knows us, and he's on to something. I say we should finish him off and get rid of the corpse."

Bourne-Atkins rushed over to them. "You callous swine! How can you say such things?"

Bill stood up and looked Bourne-Atkins in the face. "You don't know anything about us, Bourne-Atkins or whatever you call yourself. Nothing at all. If we finish him off, he'll never be found again. Never! And that means he won't talk. . . . He's the only one who knows us . . . those insurance men won't talk . . . this copper is between us and freedom. Do you realize that? One bullet through that head . . . just one. Then bury him on the moor or somewhere."

George said nothing; he felt the pulse of the policeman at his feet, then stood up. "He's nearly had it, Bill."

Bill spun the chamber of the revolver in his hand, then broke the weapon. From his pocket he produced two more rounds and slid them smoothly into position. He closed the weapon, spun the chamber and blew down the barrel.

"I'll finish him off, shall I?"

Bourne-Atkins rushed forward. "No, no! You can't!"

George put out an arm; Bourne-Atkins stopped in his tracks.

"No further, mister. You didn't see anything. Right?"

"I won't let you! Swine! You cold-blooded swine . . ." and he began to struggle fiercely with George. But George was more than a match for his ageing adversary. In a matter of seconds, he had a half-Nelson grip on the older man, holding him with his head pressed forward, facing the still, unconscious form of PC Jackson.

"I think we'd better dump him," put in George, gasping with the effort of the past few moments. "He won't talk . . . we'll scare the living daylights out of him, like we did with the others."

"Coppers don't scare that easily, George. 'Specially this one," and Bill pressed the muzzle of the barrel against the temple of Colin Jackson.

"No . . . no!" Bourne-Atkins struggled and screamed. "No!"

He lashed out with his feet, kicking George on his shins . . . he was free.

"No . . ." He threw himself across the body of the fallen constable, dragging George to the floor with him. Bill staggered back; the pistol waved in the air, and George seized Bourne-Atkins again, trying to haul him from the floor—haul him out of the way.

Bill shouted, "Bloody fools, both of you. . . ."

Bourne-Atkins fought like a madman. "I'm not having murder done before my eyes. I'm not. . . ."

Bill closed in on the older man, the pistol level. "Stand still," he bellowed. "Stand still, Bourne-Atkins and listen."

He obeyed.

Bill continued, "If that copper survives, we're all sunk. You included. You'll get time, without any doubt. I don't intend letting that happen to me, understand?" And Bill brought up the pistol and pressed it against Bourne-Atkins' head, just behind his eye.

"So," he continued, "I intend disposing of this meddlesome copper, see? And you will not stop me. We'll then get out of this place until things simmer down. Right?"

Bourne-Atkins jabbed his elbow into Bill's ribs. "I don't care what happens to me!"

Bill jerked back with the pain; there was the crash of an exploding pistol. The smoke; the smell. A cry. . . .

Bourne-Atkins fell dead across the legs of PC Jackson, blood spurting from a gaping hole in the side of his head.

George cried, "What the hell. . . ."

"He knocked me . . . hit me in the ribs . . . it went off, George . . . honest. . . ."

"God! What a bloody mess. Look at that blood!"

"Handkerchief. Bung it up with that . . . stop it flowing. . . ."

George bent down; the blood had eased to a steady flow; a river of dark, thick blood oozing from the dead man's head, running on to the coconut matting of the farmhouse floor.

Bill didn't move; the shock of the sudden discharge of his firearm had alarmed him, but the situation demanded action. And Bill wasn't afraid of action.

"George. We've done it now. What about the copper?"

"He'll have to go as well, won't he? Both of 'em."

Bill nodded. "In here?"

"Why not? Plenty of blood around. Then we'll take 'em away."

PC Jackson groaned suddenly; his right arm twitched.

"He's coming round. Let him have it, Bill."

With practised care, Bill aimed the pistol at the still form of the unconscious policeman, then moved a shade closer. He aimed for the head, the most positive place and the most vulnerable place when death was to be considered.

George, surprisingly, turned his face away.

Bill pressed the trigger. The policeman shook under the impact of the bullet; it buried itself in his brain and extinguished the flickering life that remained in the body of Police Constable Colin Jackson.

After the deed, there was deadly silence in that room. George turned to gaze down upon the scene of slaughter before him, and Bill merely blew the smoke out of the barrel of his firearm, then pushed it deep into his trouser pocket.

"We'll have to clear out now," said George.

"After we've got rid of these two," put in Bill.

"Rid of them? How?"

"Bury them on the moors."

"That'll take ages. We'll be seen. Tracks. The car . . . dogs will find them. . . ."

"We can't just leave them here? God! We can't do that!" snapped Bill. "Is there anywhere outside?"

"Plenty of buildings, but someone'll find them. If we go, folks will come prowling round the farm."

"I know!" Bill cried. "Got it! The dutch barn. In there. Put bales of hay round them. Then set fire to it. Plenty of paraffin and oil. . . ."

"Yeah! That's it. And we'll clear out as soon as we know there's a good blaze . . . before the Brigade comes."

"We won't call it!"

"Somebody will! You can bet your life on that. But we must clean up the place first; get rid of all our stuff. Wipe the place clear of fingerprints. . . ."

Bill said, "Aren't you being too careful, George?"

"No, I'm not!" bellowed the big man. "Suppose that fire leaves part of a body behind; suppose we leave a fingerprint behind? Along come the scientifics from the cops and trace us. . . . Get it?"

Bill nodded, "Have we got time though? They'll be on to us, surely?"

"Who? Who knows us? We've terrified those insurance chaps . . . that young copper would report going to Bourne-Atkins house . . . we've nicked the Wolseley from Stockton and stuck plates on it . . . we've rented this place and folk around here think we're farmers. Nobody can connect us with any of the events, Bill. So come along. Let's get this floor cleaned up. Bodies outside first, and into the dutch barn. And the last thing we do before leaving, is to set fire to it."

"Right. There's a handcart outside, for shifting muck. We can use that."

And so the two men set to work.

At about the time the first bullet thudded into the back of young PC Jackson, a dark green Ford Cortina pulled up outside Southburn Police Office. Three men climbed out; two young ones and a mature one with thick, silvery hair.

They entered the office and addressed Sergeant Bailey.

"Crime Squad. My name is Purnell. Detective Sergeant Purnell, and these are my colleagues, Detective Constables Dickinson and Arden.

"You'll have come about Bourne-Atkins?"

"Yes. Tied up with a fatal accident out Embleton way."

"Well, I can fill you in with the details so far. Come in and sit down; I'll fix a cup of coffee."

Over coffee, Sergeant Bailey told them all he knew, plus the fact that PC Jackson had traced the registration number of the blue Jaguar.

Purnell explained the latest news to Bailey—the discovery of a Jaguar behind a village pub, and the identity of the dead cyclist.

They talked for over half an hour, and eventually Purnell said, "Where is young Jackson, then?"

"He left me a note, just after nine this morning. Said he was going to ask Bourne-Atkins some more questions."

"You shouldn't have let him, Sergeant. Impetuous youth, so your Superintendent told me. Keen, but acts without thinking. He could have messed up the whole affair."

"My fault, I suppose. I was out late last night—a dinner dance at the place where my wife works. He'd gone when I got into the office."

"Not to worry. Now, we've tried to find a little more about that Bourne-Atkins. There's nothing in our files on him. I know you think he's been behaving oddly, but have you any information that might help?"

"I've told you all I know."

"Right. Now, this insurance man, Kennedy."

"Nice lad. Had one hell of a time, though."

"We'd like to speak to him."

"He's off work for a week, I understand."

"Would he talk to us?"

"I don't think he'll talk to anyone."

"But he saw the Jaguar outside Bourne-Atkins' house, didn't he? He might have seen the occupants, too. Anyway, we'll approach him. Right. First things first. I'll go and speak to Bourne-Atkins myself, straightaway. We'll go and see how your PC Jackson is coping. . . ."

"Shall I come too?"

"No. I'd rather you didn't, Mr. Bailey. Plain clothes job this."

"Fair enough. Send Jackson back, will you? I think this case is out of his hands now."

"I'll do that."

All three roared away in their Cortina and drove towards Almond Grove with Purnell at the wheel. They had no difficulty in finding the way, and pulled up outside the house.

"Arden—round the back. Don't knock and don't go in. Just see that no one leaves. Dickinson—you come in with me."

Allowing time for Arden to reach the rear of the house, Detective Sergeant Purnell strode towards the front door, with Dickinson a few paces behind.

At the door, he stopped and knocked loudly.

They waited. No reply.

"Is this the right house?" asked Dickinson.

"Number twenty-eight. That's the address Sergeant Bailey gave us."

He hammered again until the sounds echoed through the house.

"Not answering," he said. "I wonder where young Jackson's gone then?"

"I'll have a look through the window, Serge," and Dickinson moved along the stone flagged path which led from the front door, round the side until it eventually reached the rear of the premises.

He pressed his face against the window pane, shielding his eyes with his hands, and peered into the lounge.

"His cap's on the settee, Serge. The fireside rug's ruffled up, too. Looks as if there's been a struggle or something."

"That's more than bloody likely. I'm going in. Come along, follow me."

"We haven't a warrant."

"Doesn't matter. I'm using my Common Law powers to search the premises of a suspected person. That's if I'm asked. Right, in we go."

He tried the door; it opened easily.

Inside, Sergeant Purnell stopped and called, "PC Jackson? Mr. Bourne-Atkins?"

There was no reply.

"Come in, Dickinson. Close the door behind you, then nip through to the back and fetch your mate."

The detective constable did as he was told and Sergeant Purnell stood in the open doorway of the lounge, chin in hand, looking at the scene.

On the settee was a police cap, and the hearth rug had been disturbed and lay in disarray. Otherwise, the room was tidy and clean.

Only after taking a careful scrutiny from the doorway, did Purnell step in to examine the cap. He lifted it and turned it over.

Inside was Colin Jackson's name, written in ballpoint around the sweat band, and the cap bore the badge of the local constabulary. Purnell replaced it.

At this point, the two detective constables rejoined him.

"Nothing this way, serge."

"Empty as a new dustbin," commented their superior. "What do you lads make of it?"

"Jackson's been and there's been a hurried departure. He's tried to arrest someone—hence the struggle and that someone whoever he was, wasn't going to be arrested. Jackson forcibly removed. Lost his cap—door left unlocked in the rush."

"Yep. Right—upstairs now."

They searched the upstairs rooms, all tidy and clean, then the garage.

"Nobody. Right, lads. While we're here, we'll give this house a real going over. We might come across something that will tell us a little about Bourne-Atkins."

Under his orders, the detectives began their expert and methodical search.

Meanwhile Sergeant Purnell rang Southburn Office to report the suspected disappearance of PC Jackson.

In the meantime, PC Makins of Anderton had attended to the stolen car left in the yard of his local pub. The CID had come and dusted the entire vehicle for finger-prints, but reported that it had been wiped clean. Even the internal mirror, the place usually forgotten by car stealers, had been cleansed of any telltale prints, and from this it was deduced that the vehicle had been in the hands of expert criminals.

The Information Room check on its number showed it had, in fact, been stolen from a Lincolnshire village some three months ago.

And now, after the scientific examination had been concluded, it was arranged that one of the CID men should drive it past Hive Cottage, Drydale, so that Henry Simmons could identify it.

If he did, the dead cyclist and the Jaguar could be linked; the car and two men could be linked; No. 28 Almond Grove and Mr. Bourne-Atkins could also be linked.

But linked to what? Or for what reason?

The CID men who had investigated the Jaguar, downed a couple of quick pints each, then radioed their results to their force Information Room, asking that the Crime Squad be informed.

And at that stage, all the links in the chain were joined. It only remained to see where the chain ended.

Back at No. 28 Almond Grove, the search had revealed a good deal. In an old suitcase on top of a wardrobe in the spare bedroom, Sergeant Purnell had found lots to interest him.

There were family photograph albums, snap shots, newspaper cuttings and other personal items of family interest. And among them was a file of newspaper cuttings, giving details of a man called Joseph Shadwell; he'd owned a village store; he'd been elected as a county councillor and lived in a Midland village called Fairthorpe; played for the cricket team; opened a larger shop in Wolverhampton; general grocers. Then bought a TV and radio shop as well; ran the pair of them. He still lived in Fairthorpe. They found a photograph in a local paper. It was a picture of Joe Shadwell winning a cup for the best all-round performance in 1957. Some years ago. . . .

Then a cutting at the bottom of the pile. A loose one.

"Shadwell Guilty of Receiving Stolen Property," ran the banner headline.

"I think this is it, lads," chuckled Sergeant Purnell. "I think our Mr. Bourne-Atkins is Joe Shadwell. Let's find out, shall we?"

11

SERGEANT PURNELL rang the village policeman at Fairthorpe, which lay a few miles from the boundaries of Wolverhampton, and he used the telephone in Bourne-Atkins' house.

"Tees-side Crime Squad," he announced himself. "Detective Sergeant Purnell speaking." And then he outlined his queries about the man known as Shadwell.

The village bobby listened carefully, and when the sergeant had finished his story, the bobby spoke.

"Shadwell lived here until three or four years ago; he got convicted for that receiving job you mentioned. It certainly hit the headlines of the local press, sergeant, because of his influential position in the village. On top of that, his wife died, too—suspected cancer. Personally, I think the disgrace finished her off. Nice woman. Anyway, Shadwell left here. No one knows where he went. He's never been seen since."

"You'll have a criminal record of him down there?"

"Wolverhampton have got it, sergeant. The conviction was in respect of premises within their city boundaries. The stolen stuff was found there."

"OK. I'd like a photograph rushed up here, and fingerprint records, too."

"Look," said the village constable. "I'm going into Wolverhampton office now—I'll ring them first and ask them to get the stuff out. Will it do by post?"

"Quicker if possible. There's a good rail service from your part of the world to Leeds; we can arrange collection there. Could you fix that?"

"Sure. I'll ring back with train times."

"Ring Southburn office, please," and he gave the number. "Shadwell's got himself mixed up with something here—we want him positively identified as soon as possible. Goes by the name of Bourne-Atkins here."

"Does he? Posh eh? He had a good business down here. . . ."

"Pity he fell, eh? Anyway, you'll fix things for me?"

"Sure, sergeant. Cheerio."

Sergeant Purnell rubbed his hands with delight. This was the sort of enquiry he enjoyed—already, things were moving and he was unearthing useful information.

He instructed his men to gather all the documents and cuttings which might be relevant, and occupied himself downstairs by searching for fingerprints which might be useful to prove conclusively the identity of the man who lived here.

The bathroom; always a likely source of fingerprints. There was a wall cabinet with a mirror door and as he switched on the light, Purnell saw several good prints on the glass. They must be preserved; they would be compared with the ones being rushed up from Wolverhampton. They might prove Shadwell was Bourne-Atkins.

Then the telephone rang.

"I'll get it," he shouted, and he answered it by giving the number written on the disc on the telephone.

"Sergeant Purnell?" asked a voice.

"Speaking."

"Bailey here, Southburn."

"Yes, Mr. Bailey."

"That message you passed earlier, about young Jackson. Has he come back yet?"

"No. Not a sign of him. Why?"

"Well, he's not here. Wonder where on earth he's got to? I'm worried. I mean, those thugs have beaten up two men already—think what they might do to a copper who's on to them."

"You'll have told your boss about it?"

"I rang him immediately I heard from you."

"What did he say?"

"Give him an hour," replied Sergeant Bailey. "He said give him an hour. Look —could you ask at the houses next door? They might have seen something."

"Yes. Don't go away. You'll be getting

a call from Wolverhampton." Purnell explained the reason for that call.

After speaking to Bailey, he shouted for Arden.

"Arden. House-to-house enquiries here, please. PC Jackson came here shortly after nine. He's not been seen since. Ask around, will you?"

Arden let himself out of the front door, and Sergeant Purnell gathered the evidence into his arms.

"I'm taking this lot to Southburn Office, Dickinson. Hang on here, will you? Someone might ring, or call."

Dickinson nodded his agreement, and Purnell said, "Afterwards, I'm going to see that youth, Kennedy. If you want me, ring Southburn office from this house."

"Right ho, Serge." And Detective Constable Dickinson settled down to a long, boring wait.

Purnell, fired with the success of the past hour, left the suitcase of documents at Southburn Police Station, discovered the whereabouts of Kennedy's home, and drove round to Iburndale Terrace.

He found forty-seven, clean and inviting, and rang the bell. A smart young woman answered the door; she didn't smile and had a distinct appearance of apprehension on her face.

"Mrs. Kennedy?"

"Yes?"

"My name is Purnell. Detective Sergeant Purnell from the Tees-side Crime Squad. I'd like to speak to your husband."

She hesitated, and glanced over her shoulder; Purnell said, "I know what he's been through. Please tell him it's all right. It is important, otherwise I shouldn't have come."

"I'll ask him." And she disappeared inside, leaving the door ajar.

A smart house; colourful inside and carefully cleaned. The home of a young married couple.

Then she was returning.

"Come in, Sergeant," she invited. "That door on the right. The lounge."

Purnell obeyed. In the lounge he found a tall, handsome young man; at least he would be handsome if his eyes and lips were normal. Heavy blue bruises showed around his mouth and his eyes were yellowing and purple.

"Hello," greeted Purnell. "Mr. Kennedy?"

The man nodded and extended his hand.

"You have had a thumping haven't you? Feeling better?"

"I'm aching like hell all over, but I'll be fine. Who are you?"

"Sorry. I thought your wife told you. The name is Purnell. I'm a Detective Sergeant from Tees-side Crime Squad." Purnell produced his warrant card from his pocket and showed it to Kennedy.

"All right. But I'm not saying anything, Sergeant. I daren't."

"I realize what you've been through, Mr. Kennedy. I know what this sort of person is capable of doing and I respect your fears for your wife and home. Nonetheless, I had to come and talk to you. It's vital."

"Sit down, but you're wasting your time."

Mrs. Kennedy came into the room.

Purnell settled himself on the edge of an armchair, and wondered how to begin questioning this youthful man.

"I think," he began, "that I must put you in the picture entirely. I'll tell you everything."

And he told everything that he knew or suspected, re-living Henry Simmons' moments as he knocked down an unknown cyclist, and continuing up to the current time.

"And now," he concluded, "PC Jackson has vanished. We think they've got him."

Mrs. Kennedy cried, "Not that nice young policeman who called here? The one who brought Jim's car back?"

"That'll be him. He's been reported missing, Mrs. Kennedy; we can't find that man Bourne-Atkins, or Shadwell, as he is most probably called. Jackson went to the house where you saw the Jaguar and he's vanished."

"But why? What's going on?" asked Mrs. Kennedy.

"If we knew that, we'd be a long way towards finding our villains," said Purnell. "And that is why I've come back here, to talk to your husband."

"But look what they did to me! Look! And they threatened June, and my baby . . . and the house. If I talk to the police, they'll kill me. . . ."

"Did they say that?"

"No, but they will, won't they? The mood they were in. . . ."

"Suppose we gave you police protection —permanently I mean, until we get them behind bars."

"But you can't protect us all the time . . . June has to go shopping . . . I'll go to work next week. . . ."

"Tell you what," said Purnell. "Have you a spare room?"

Mrs. Kennedy spoke. "A little room at the back. It's a junk room at the moment."

"Suppose I got a detective to live here . . . as a lodger. Would you be agreeable to that? You see, you are one of the few people who saw those men, Mr. Kennedy. You can describe them. We desperately need your help. PC Jackson needs your help."

"I know . . . I know! But good God, Sergeant. Suppose I help you; suppose you catch them . . . I'll have to go to court as a witness and they'll know I've talked to you. What will they do then? They'll come round here and half kill me. God knows what they'll do to June and the baby!"

"Mr. Kennedy, I've been in the police force a long, long time. Probably since you were born. Over twenty years, in fact. I've come across this problem again and again—it's a common event, you know. Witnesses are threatened with personal violence if they talk to us. And in spite of that, witnesses have talked to us, and never to my knowledge, have they subsequently been harmed. Not once. Look at it this way—if you will not tell us what happened, or what you saw the other day, these men might escape for

191

ever. We might never catch them. If that is so, they will remain free for ever which in turn means that you will be always in fear of them. Fear for yourself and for your family. You'll never be free from that fear as long as you live. If you talk to me, and give me the details I ask for, you will help us to put these men behind bars. I will do my utmost to see that you are not brought forward as a witness against them—and I will ensure that they never know that you have talked. Think now of that young policeman. Where is he? We know that two men and Bourne-Atkins are involved. We know enough about Bourne-Atkins to trace him, but we know nothing about the other two. Nothing at all. As I told you earlier, they dumped the Jaguar. We haven't a cat-in-hell's chance of finding them. So I repeat my offer—if you have a spare room and a bed, I can arrange for a detective to stay with you, in the house. For a week to start with. After that we'll see how things are. He will live here, work here and accompany your wife when she goes out. She can say it's a cousin or something."

June Kennedy spoke. "We've got a bed, but no blankets or sheets. Can't afford such things yet . . . not for a spare bed."

"I could fix that. How about it then?"

Kennedy looked at the carpet, his hands clasped tight before him, gripping until the whites of his knuckles showed against the tightness of his joints.

"Jim," said his wife, "tell the Sergeant."

"But you. . . ."

"I'm willing to have a detective living here for a while."

"But it's so risky . . . so bloody terrifying. . . ."

"I know. I know only too well," said Purnell. "It's happened to me, too."

Kennedy looked up at him. "What happened in your case?"

"I discovered that four men were running a brothel on Tees-side—taking young girls and forcing them into becoming prostitutes. They were making a fortune from foreign seamen . . . all those men ran sports cars. I was a young copper—about your age—and I had a wife and two children. Twins. They found out where I lived. Threatened my wife and kids, just like you, if I didn't stop my enquiries."

"Did you stop?"

"No. I got them all put behind bars."

"Did they hurt your family?"

"We got threatening phone calls; my wife got a couple of anonymous letters threatening to hurt her and the twins, and six of our windows were smashed one night."

"But you continued?"

"I had to, hadn't I? It's a psychological thing, really. These sort of people are bullies, and as long as they get their own way, they will continue to bully. But if someone hits back at a bully, he will back down. So I hit back. Hard. Now, threats don't frighten me any more, and thank God, they don't frighten my wife either."

Kennedy spoke. "I see your point. They were bullies. Two of them on to me

. . . bastards! All right, Sergeant. I'll tell you what I know—but you will arrange for someone to look after June, please?"

"If you've a telephone, I'll ring now."

"Help yourself. It's in the next room."

Purnell rang his Headquarters, and returned five minutes later.

"That's fixed. A policewoman is on her way now . . ."

"Policewoman!" shrieked Kennedy.

"A detective—plain clothes girl. Don't worry. She's the best we have. Came second this year in the National Policewoman's Judo Championships. Crack shot with a pistol. She'll bring a firearm with her, just in case. She's worth six normal coppers is this girl. Mary Anderson. You'll like her."

"I'm looking forward to her coming!" said June Kennedy. "I'll go and fix the room. She's bringing sheets?"

"She'll bring everything she needs."

"I didn't expect a girl, Sergeant," said Kennedy when June had gone. "It's unusual, isn't it?"

"Exactly. If—and I repeat if—they do

come to attack you, they won't expect a girl, either, will they? They'll dismiss her as a relation . . . and what a damned shock they'll have."

Kennedy smiled for the first time and said, "Thanks a million. Right. I'll tell you what happened."

"Thanks."

And the two men settled down for a long chat. Kennedy was at ease now, and Purnell knew the talk would do him a world of good. It would get rid of the fear that was in his system.

Henry Simmons waited at his window with Margaret at his elbow. Embleton Police had telephoned to say they intended driving the blue Jaguar past his house at about eleven.

They had told him the registration number did not correspond with the one seen by him, but after consultation with Southburn police, they now knew the number was false. However, to give the Jaguar the appearance it had that night, they had built a set of false plates, corresponding to those carried by the car before its recovery, and it was these plates the car bore as it drove towards Drydale.

The grandfather clock in the dining-room struck eleven.

"Any time now," said Margaret, clutching his arm tightly.

"I wonder if it is the one," he half whispered.

"They've never been back. Those men, I mean."

"I don't suppose they will now. They'll never give evidence for me, but the police are interested in something else, obviously."

"Are you frightened, Henry? After their threats, I mean?"

"I'm worried for your sake, darling—and the children. But PC Christian reassured me when he rang this morning. Apparently, there are lots of threats like this, and few of them are carried out."

"I think it's coming," cried Margaret, pointing along the village street. "I saw a flash of blue between those houses at the top end."

"Right. Let me have a good look."

Henry leaned forward and saw the moving car.

"It's a blue Jaguar all right. Has it got a dented mudguard at the front—the far side from us?"

"Can't see," replied his wife.

"It's coming slowly," he said. "Here it is . . . ah. There! See that mudguard on the far side—the off-side of the car. Dented and covered in dark green paint. To stop it rusting till they get it repaired . . . now, the number."

At no more than ten miles an hour, the blue Jaguar cruised through Drydale, and now it was opposite Hive Cottage. Henry watched with his hands clutching the window frame and then it was past.

He saw the number PDF40Q.

"I'm sure it's the car," he spoke softly, almost to himself. "I thought it said 400 in the dark."

"You could mistake a 'Q' for an 'O'," she said.

"I could. Otherwise, I'd swear it was the same car."

"What do you have to do now?"

"They'll ring me from Embleton to ask my opinion. I'll just have to wait now. I'm sure it's the same car."

"Do you think the police will get the men?"

"I expect so. But it's no concern of mine now, is it? I can forget them as defence witnesses. It's a criminal job now, and PC Christian said the crime squad was dealing with it."

"They won't want you any more, will they?"

"Not now," said Henry Simmons. "All I have to do is wait for the Superintendent to decide about proceedings against me."

Then the telephone rang in the hall.

"I'll get it," he said. "It'll be Embleton Police checking about the car."

He picked up the receiver and said, "Simmons speaking."

A low voice said, "It's your visitors, mister. Just checking that you haven't done anything stupid, like informing the police."

12

IN the farmhouse, George replaced his telephone and grinned at Bill.

"That's put the fear of God into him! Now, what was that other insurance man's name?"

"Kennedy," said Bill, who was swilling the stone-flagged floor of the farm with copious buckets of water. "Lives in Southburn—Iburndale Terrace."

"I'll ring him as well. Have we much left to do?"

"It'll take ages to get the blood cleaned off these flags, George. Then we've got to go over the whole house and clean off fingerprints; we've a barn to clear as well, if we can. Then we have to make sure the dutch barn is safely on fire before we go."

"Are those bodies hidden sufficiently?"

"No one will find them, if that's what's worrying you. They're deep in the straw, well hidden."

George nodded with satisfaction. "Then we needn't panic, need we?"

"Panic?"

"Well, we needn't panic ourselves into rushing headlong out of here now. I think we should take our time in seeing that everything is cleansed—if we panic, we'll leave something out."

"But you don't intend staying here after today, surely?"

"Good Lord, no. It's only eleven o'clock now. Let's hide that Wolseley in one of the outbuildings; I suppose it will have been reported as stolen by now."

"It's got false plates on."

"I know, but the cops will be seeking a black Wolseley, stolen from Stockton-on-Tees. And this is a special sort of car, isn't it? We were daft to take this one."

"There wasn't anything else handy. I'll hide it," agreed Bill, "while you ring Kennedy. Are you sure the calls won't be traced?"

"Impossible. I just dial his number, say my bit and slap down my telephone. He knows who called, and it'll just remind him not to talk."

"He saw us, you know. Could recognize us."

"But the cops have nothing on us, have they? Nothing. Right, you move the car. I'll ring him and then we'll get this floor finished."

Bill left his washing activities and went outside, as George looked up Kennedy's number in the directory which lay on the window ledge of the lounge of the farm.

Minutes later he was dialling the number.

"Darling," shouted June Kennedy from the toe of the stairs, "can you help me turn this mattress, please? I want to give that policewoman a comfy bed."

"Coming," he said, and then, "Excuse me, Sergeant. Domestic business; back in a tick."

Purnell listened as the young insurance agent clumped upstairs, and heard him walk across the floor above him.

Then the telephone rang.

"I'll get it!" cried Sergeant Purnell. "Might be for me, anyway."

"Thanks," came the muffled response from upstairs, and Purnell made his way to the ringing telephone.

He lifted it up and announced himself by reading the telephone number.

Then a voice said, "It's your fighters, mister. Just checking that you haven't done anything stupid, like informing the cops."

Purnell caught his breath. He didn't reply. He held the telephone close to his ear, listening for background sounds, for some hint of the caller's origin. . . .

A car, roaring; hens clucking, in startled fright.

Then a click and the line went dead.

Kennedy was coming downstairs, and Purnell went to meet him.

"It was for me," he said. "Routine stuff."

Kennedy nodded; Purnell had no intention of telling him about the call because, currently, he was getting along fine with this youngster and his wife.

"Right. Can we continue?" asked Purnell.

They returned to the lounge and Purnell continued with his questioning.

"Well, now. These two men," he said. "Can we go over their descriptions again?"

Kennedy nodded and repeated his description.

"The big one was called George. Smartly dressed, I'd say. But big and hellish strong. Plenty of dark hair."

"Accents?"

"Nothing I could place. Well spoken, almost."

"Anything distinctive about him? Did he have a habit that you noticed? Blinking his eyes, or some gesture with his hands?"

"No. Can't say I noticed . . . oh, there was one thing. He kept saying 'Mister' after almost every sentence."

The caller on the telephone had said Mister, recalled Purnell.

"Was it noticeable to any degree?"

"I think so. It stuck out in my mind.

Although I wasn't in their company for long—happily for me—I reached the stage where I could guess when he was going to say 'Mister' again."

"Thanks. This is useful information, believe it or not. Our Criminal Records Offices keep a log of these habits. We've been able to identify criminals because of them. I'll check on this in a moment. Now, the other one?"

"Bill. He was the car driver. Wonderful control he had—I'd guess he'd make a first rate rally driver. Slim build. Fairer hair than George. Smart as well."

"Age?"

"Like George. Early to middle thirties."

"Scars? Mannerisms?"

"Nothing I can recall. George seemed to be the boss of the pair, although he wasn't bossy. I suppose a better word is 'Leader'."

"I follow." Purnell had been jotting down these brief word-portraits. "Can I use your phone again? I want to get a check made on these men as soon as I can."

"Sure."

Purnell rang his own office in Middlesbrough.

"Purnell here. Can you do a character check for me, Jack? With NECRO? Right. Man; christian name George. In his thirties, smartly dressed, uses word 'mister' after lots of his sentences. Dark hair. Height? Hang on."

"Six feet," called Kennedy.

"Six feet," repeated Purnell into the telephone. "His mate is Bill. Shorter than George . . ."

"Five-seven," said Kennedy.

"Five foot seven inches," responded Purnell. "Lighter hair, same age group. Smartly dressed, too. Expert car driver."

There was silence, and then Purnell said, "If you get anything in the next half hour, ring this number," and he gave Kennedy's number. "If I've gone, I'll ring you sometime. Heard from Dickinson or Arden at all?"

The response was negative and Purnell put down the receiver.

"Right," he said. "That's started the identification chain. It's not much, but at least it's a start."

"Can you identify men from as little as that?" asked Kennedy.

"Sometimes less. We know them by their habits, their way of working, their preference in cars, pubs, beer, women . . . it takes all sorts to make the criminal fraternity. Believe it or not, some crooks leave visiting cards, as the Saint does. I once got a chap identified because he snapped his fingers every time he spoke to a woman . . . a nervous habit he'd picked up."

"And are all these indexed?"

"As far as we can. Your word 'mister' will be indexed under that word if this chap George has been through our hands before. And against it, there will be his name. If we get that, all we have to do is to locate him."

"That won't be easy."

"But it won't be impossible,"

commented Purnell. "Right, Mr. Kennedy. I think I've got all I need for the time being. You've been most helpful to me and I appreciate how difficult it must be to talk to me in the circumstances. That policewoman is on her way now, and until she arrives, we'll go over what you've already told me. We'll do it like this—I'll tell you what I've learned, and you correct me if I'm wrong, or if there's any important point missing. Anything you think should be in will be included—we must get these men."

"OK."

And they settled down again.

"Who was that?" asked Margaret Simmons as Henry returned.

"Wrong number," he lied easily.

"I thought it was a short call."

Then it rang again, and Henry hesitated; Margaret said, "Aren't you going to answer it? It'll be the Police."

He didn't answer, but moved once more into the hall and lifted the receiver.

"PC Christian here," came the voice. "Everything all right, Mr. Simmons?"

"Er . . . yes. Yes. All fine." He didn't want to mention that call because it would alarm his wife. "The Jaguar has been past."

"And?"

"It's the one." Henry had said it; that telephone call wasn't going to terrify him. If he grew more frightened, his fear would affect Margaret, and then the children . . . besides, he had police protection.

"You sure?" came the voice of PC Christian.

"I had a good look at the front, Mr. Christian. It's the car, but I wouldn't swear to the number. This one is 40Q—I thought I saw 400, but, of course, it was dark and raining at the time."

"Fair enough," said Christian. "You know the Crime Squad is on to the job now? I don't know what aspect they're investigating, but you've stirred something up."

"Sorry. If I hadn't. . . ."

"Don't be sorry. You've probably prevented a lot of people from getting hurt."

"I suppose that's one way of looking at it," said Henry. "What happens now?"

"So far as you are concerned, not a great lot. We're opening the inquest for identification of the cyclist—you won't be required for that. Then it will be adjourned until your court case has been heard."

"Then there is to be a case?"

"I'm jumping the gun," admitted Christian. "I was talking in a procedural sort of way, but you see my point?"

"I do. When will I know?"

"A day or two, I expect."

"Thanks," and they rang off.

Henry returned to his wife and managed a smile for her.

"It was the car, I'm sure," he said. "Wish they'd hurry up with the decision about my accident."

"Have they heard any more about those awful men?" asked Margaret.

He shook his head. "They did say the Crime Squad was looking into things."

She linked her arm in his and said, "Well, at least we can relax again, can't we? Fancy a cup of coffee?"

"Love one, darling," he said. "Then I'd better have a walk round the village to collect a few premiums."

Sergeant Purnell drove back to Southburn Police Office in a thoughtful mood. Young Jim Kennedy had talked well, and he had provided some useful information.

How was Dickinson getting along? Still waiting at the house in Almond Grove? And Arden, doing house to house enquiries to see if anyone had seen anything this morning.

PC Jackson? Where was he?

Then there was that dead cyclist, lying in Embleton mortuary. How was he connected with George and Bill? Was there in fact any connection between them? If so, what were they doing? Bourne-Atkins, alias Shadwell—how did he fit into the scheme of things?

He suddenly decided to return to the house.

Detective Constable Dickinson was still there, and opened the door to his Sergeant.

"Hello, Serge. Nothing doing."

"Looks as though they've skipped, doesn't it? Seen Arden?"

"Not since you left."

"Wait here till twelve-thirty, then. If Arden calls here, send him round to Southburn Police Station; in fact, come with him. We'll hold a conference to decide what to do next."

"Right."

Leaving his men to their mundane tasks, Purnell finally drove to the police station in Southburn.

"Ah," said Sergeant Bailey. "Your office has been ringing for you."

"Here?"

"They rang Kennedy's house just after you left; he said they'd find you here."

"I'll ring them."

Purnell dialled the number and spoke

to one of his colleagues. "Purnell here, Jack. You wanted me?"

"Yes. Those two characters you want identifying. We've got them on our lists."

"Have we! Ruddy marvellous. What news?"

"It was that word 'mister' that did it. George is George Edwin Shaw, thirty-five years old, described as a farmer, five feet eleven inches tall, dark brown hair, going thin on top, born in Birmingham. His home address is given as Manor Farm, Waupley, Nottinghamshire, but I haven't checked down there yet."

"He's obviously got convictions. What sort are they?"

"Mixed bag. Larceny, receiving stolen property, demanding with menaces. . . ."

"Demanding with menaces, eh? Black-mailer? That's interesting."

"That explains a lot, I suppose. His last one, by the way, was only three months ago. A parking offence in Sunderland."

"Sunderland! I wonder if he's been in this part of the world since then?"

"It's a thought, Serge. If so, where's he living?"

"A good question. Is he wanted for any outstanding offences?"

"Not that we know of."

"Good. Now, his mate?"

"The one called Bill. He seems certain to be William Bowry, described as an electrician and a frequent companion of Shaw's. Thirty-one years old, 5′ 8″, black hair, born at Sandhurst. He's got convictions for burglary, office breaking, shop breaking and garage breaking, plus a couple for dangerous driving and one for taking motor vehicles without the owners' consent."

"A pair of likely lads. Did you get this information from NECRO?"

"Yes. And they've got photographs. I've asked them to send copies here immediately."

"Well done. What time will they arrive?"

"Not later than two o'clock this afternoon—at the Middlesbrough office."

"Can you fetch them to Southburn? I want a chap to have a look at them."

"Will do, Serge."

"Thanks. Right, now. Ring Nottinghamshire, will you? Check that address—Manor Farm, Waupley. See what they can tell us about this character. And before you do that, ring Embleton, Jack. They've got a dead cyclist in their morgue—chap called Edmunds. Tell Embleton Police what you've discovered, and then see if Nottingham can connect Edmunds with our two rogues. Is that clear?"

"Sure. You'll ring here?"

"I'll be in touch, Jack. Well done. Things are moving now. Get those photographs over here as soon as you can. A local copper is missing here—got the cars looking for him. We think they must have got him."

"Poor devil! I'll do my best."

And Jack rang off.

Sergeant Purnell settled down into a chair and took out his pipe. It was the first chance he'd had to light it, and to relax since this morning.

As he lit it, Sergeant Bailey came through from his office, bearing a cup of steaming coffee.

"Like this?" he said. "You sound as if you've been busy."

"I have," he said, and as he drank the coffee, the two sergeants talked about the case so far.

"It's my belief," said Purnell at last, "that these characters have been spending a lot of time in this part of England—the North East, I mean."

"Doing what?"

"Something criminal. How about demanding with menaces?"

"It sounds their sort of game."

"Yes. Or receiving stolen property—maybe both. That cyclist might have been with them—part of the set-up. By getting himself killed, he's upset their applecart a little, and things have started to go wrong."

"Feasible," acknowledged Bailey. "Can we connect any of these men with any certainty?"

"Not yet. And your chap here—

Bourne-Atkins, alias Shadwell—where does he fit into the scheme of things?"

"He's got a conviction for receiving stolen property, hasn't he?"

"Blimey! I'd forgotten that. That cyclist—Edmunds. Has he?"

"You'll have to ring Embleton about that. They've got details on their files."

"Thanks. You know, we might check the actual dates of the convictions for receiving for each man. If they are at the same court at the same time, there's our connection!"

"That's it!" grinned Bailey. "Will you do that?"

"Leave it to me. Now, this lad Jackson. Any news?"

"I'm sitting here like a twit, just waiting. We've got all our men out looking for him. But, so far, not a whisper."

"Is he married?"

"No. In a way, it's a blessing. At least, I don't have the worry of a panicking wife on my hands."

"My lad, Arden, is asking questions

about him. He's knocking about that housing estate—I've left instructions for him to call back here. You might ask him what he's learned, if I'm not around."

"Sure. You going out?"

"Not just yet. In fact, I'm wondering where to turn now. I've seen Kennedy . . . funny, you know. There was a phone call for him whilst I was there. I answered it. It was those bloody rogues—threatening him again."

"You took it?"

"He was upstairs. I pretended the call was for me, so he doesn't know they're still trying to keep him quiet. Good lad, that. . . ."

"Who made it?"

"George—George Edwin Shaw, as we now know him—he called me Mister and he thought he was talking to Kennedy."

"Where did he ring from?"

"No idea. It certainly wasn't a kiosk, or I'd have heard the coins dropping, or the STD tone . . . I listened for background noises. Heard a car. . . ."

"A car?"

"Hey! Wait a minute. A car. And hens. Hens frightened by a car, cackling . . . a farm!"

"Farm?"

"He's a farmer, isn't he? Shaw is listed as a farmer! On his conviction card! I want a list of every farm for miles around which has recently changed hands!"

13

IN the meantime, Detective Constable Paul Arden had knocked on countless doors in the Almond Grove area. Most of the residents who were at home at this time of the day were either women or elderly people, although he did come across one or two men who were waiting to go on late shift.

But no one had seen anything.

No one had taken any notice of the comings and goings at number twenty-eight; cars came and cars went along the road all day and one extra car made not the slightest impression upon the local residents.

But one house had produced no response at all, and that house had annoyed Paul Arden. It was a semi-detached house, brick-built, and it stood almost opposite number twenty-eight. He had returned to it time and time again, and received no reply.

Yet there was smoke coming out of the chimney; one set of the upstairs curtains was still closed and he knew that there was someone inside. Why didn't they answer him?

It might be a man on nights, sleeping after a busy shift; it might be a young couple enjoying the fruits of wedded bliss; it might be a lazy person. Or a frightened person.

But for Detective Constable Paul Arden, such problems presented a challenge. He knew from past experience that it was this sort of house, this sort of person, which produced the goods. The one place you didn't visit would be the one which had something to offer, and he therefore made a mental note to return to this particular house after he had exhausted enquiries in the estate.

It was nearing twelve noon when he achieved this; as he walked towards number twenty-eight, tired and bored after a fruitless morning, he saw a woman with a shopping bag. She was walking up the garden path towards that brick-built house with the drawn curtains, and he increased his pace.

A woman who had been out shopping. She must have left her home fairly early. Had she seen PC Jackson? Had she seen activity at number twenty-eight?

Three minutes later he was knocking on the door yet again, and this time he produced results.

"Yes?" a young woman appeared, still dressed in her coat.

"I am a police officer," he announced. "I'd like to ask you some questions, please—I'm asking at every house in the estate."

"Oh. Well, come in. Have you called before? I've been out shopping."

He followed her into the smart house, warm and friendly, and she showed him into the lounge.

Moments later she returned, minus her coat and smiled at him.

"Well," she grinned. "What's happened? Something exciting?"

Arden returned her smile. A pleasant girl, he felt.

"Could well be," he replied. "It's that house opposite. Number twenty-eight. A Mr. Bourne-Atkins lives there."

"By himself. I've seen the gentleman around, although I don't really know him."

"Did you see him this morning?"

"Yes. Just before I went out shopping."

"Good. You're the only person who's seen anything. What time was this?"

"Not long after nine o'clock. I was upstairs, getting ready to go out. I looked out of the bedroom window."

"But the curtains are drawn," commented Arden.

She grinned. "You're quick. I slept in the other front room—the one with the open curtains. My husband's asleep in the one you're thinking about—he was on nights last night."

"Touché!" grinned Arden. "Right. What did you see?"

"Well, maybe I was being nosy, but. . . ."

"You might save a life by being nosy, Mrs. . . . er . . ."

"Campbell."

"Mrs. Campbell. What did you see?"

"Quite honestly, I don't know. To me, it looked like a fight. . . ."

"A fight?"

"Yes. In that front room of number twenty-eight. From our bedroom I can see right into that room—those big windows make that possible, you know."

"I know. What was going on?"

"I saw Mr. Bourne-Atkins and there were three other men in the room, all pushing and shoving and, well, I wondered what they were arguing about."

"Three other men?"

"Yes. One had a uniform on—like a postman, I thought."

"Go on."

"Well, naturally, I watched them."

"You wouldn't have been normal if you hadn't!" put in Arden by way of encouragement.

"They moved out of my sight, towards the right hand end of the house."

"Towards the front door?"

"That direction, but still in the room. Then the postman, or whoever he was, was on the floor. Lying there. They came with a coat and covered him up."

"Covered him up?"

"Well, something like that. Well, as you can imagine, I thought it was a funny going on. I thought he was play acting, maybe. Rehearsing for a pantomime . . . well, I had no idea. . . ."

"What happened next?"

"Nothing for a minute or so, then they all came out."

"All of them?"

"Yes. The postman had a macintosh on, and the others were carrying him, sort of."

"Carrying him? Was he ill then?"

"Drunk he looked like to me. You know, one man on either side holding an arm, supporting him. Then the last man came out and shut the door."

"Where did they go?"

"Into a car parked outside. Right opposite my house, but on the other side of the road from us."

"They all got in the car?"

"Yes, two in the front and two in the back."

"Were they still fighting, or skylarking, whatever it was."

"No, but Mr. Bourne-Atkins didn't look too happy. I could see his face quite clearly—he looked frightened, I thought."

"What about the man in the macintosh then? How did he look?"

"I couldn't see his face. His head was flopping forward, if you understand. And the two men were very close to him."

"I see. Then what?"

"Mr. Bourne-Atkins was in the front—but he wasn't driving. And the man in the macintosh was in the back. The other two men got in and the car drove away."

"Which way?"

"Towards the main road. I don't know which way it went after that."

"Now. The car. What sort was it?"

"A black one."

"Black! Make?"

"I haven't the foggiest idea. I'm hopeless when it comes to cars."

"Mmm. This is important . . ."

"It looked like one of those that you see in old Scotland Yard films—the black police cars. It was just like that."

"Was it a police car?" he asked suddenly.

"Oh, no. But it was that sort, if you understand. I could just imagine it turning into Scotland Yard—well, the old Scotland Yard. They've got a new place now, haven't they?"

"They have—and new cars, too. But I know the sort of car. They used Wolseleys."

"I don't know the makes," she said quietly.

"What did you think was happening out there?" Arden asked her.

"I don't know. I came downstairs when they'd driven off, and sat down because I was worried. Then I thought it must be a family row, maybe, and nothing to do with me. I was going to tell Alec—that's my husband—but he was asleep, so I left it. Then I had a think just now, while I was shopping and thought I'd ask Alec what to do."

"Then I came?"

"Yes. What's going on?" she asked.

"Quite frankly, I don't know," said Arden. "But that postman, as you call him, was probably one of our men."

"A policeman?"

"Yes. PC Jackson."

"Isn't he our new policeman?"

"He hasn't been here long, but he came to the house opposite to ask questions shortly after nine this morning."

"I don't know him . . . but it's dark inside . . . he looked just like, well, a postman, or a bus driver without his hat on."

"I appreciate that. Now, Mrs. Campbell, would you know those men again?"

"I don't know. But I thought they were the men who have been coming here lately, but last time they used a big blue car with a long nose."

"The same men?"

"Yes, I'm sure of it. They've been here a lot lately—in the last month or so and I thought it can't be them again because of the blue car. It was a beauty."

"I see. Well, thanks a lot, Mrs. Campbell. This is wonderful. I might want to see you again, to ask more questions."

"I'm usually about the place," she said. "How exciting . . . I might have seen a crime. . . ."

"Yes, you might indeed." He didn't speak these words aloud, but said, "Thanks for your help. If anything else comes to mind, let me know. You can contact me through Southburn Police station. Detective Constable Arden is the name."

He got up and made for the door. She came with him, and saw him out.

Arden walked across the road to number twenty-eight, spoke briefly to his mate, Dickinson, at the house, and they both left together to walk back to the local police station.

Sergeant Purnell would be interested to hear what they had learned.

"Where can I find out about farms recently let?" asked Purnell. "I'd swear I heard farmyard noises. Hens scattering as a car drove through them . . . you don't find hens running loose in towns or in gardens, do you? And he is a farmer. . . ."

"There are all the estate agents in town," said Bailey. "But it will take ages to search their records, especially as they would have to go back several months, surely?"

"Shaw's last conviction was three months ago at Sunderland, so it's a fair bet he was living somewhere near here at that time. Sunderland's just over an hour away."

"Telephone directory!" said Bailey. "See if he's in that—you said he'd telephoned from a private number."

"Got one handy?"

Bailey reached a copy from the shelves in the office and passed it to his companion who flicked through its pages.

"Shaw," he muttered to himself. "Shaw. G. E. Shaw. Ah!" he'd found the name. "W. Shaw . . . T. Shaw . . . T. A. Shaw . . . Norman Shaw, Dental Surgeon . . . G. Shaw, Tobacconist . . . Benjamin Shaw . . . No. Not here."

"That directory was published last year. February."

"So it's roughly a year old. How big an area does it cover?"

"Almost the whole of this region. Anywhere within an hour's driving distance, but give Directory Enquiries a ring. Ask if there is a G. E. Shaw on the subscription list. Ask about neighbouring telephone areas, too."

"And recent alterations to their list. I'll do it now."

Purnell reached for the telephone and rang Directory Enquiries. He explained his query and informed the operator that he was a police officer.

She promised attention immediately

and while he waited she checked all neighbouring telephone directories, and the new subscribers' list.

Within four or five minutes she returned to him.

"There is a G. A. Shaw in the York area—a ladies hairdresser."

"G. E. Shaw, farmer, is the one I'm seeking," he said. "Have you checked your new subscribers?"

"Yes, there is no such person on that list."

"But surely, if a person moves into a house with a telephone, they will ask that your records be changed? Besides, if the account goes out for payment, you'll know who pays it?"

"Not always," replied the girl on the line. "If a person takes a house temporarily, for example, they may not bother to inform us. They can ring friends from the telephone and these friends will be told their number, often without any notification being received here. As for paying the bills, this can be done by cash at any post office, you know."

"Of course. Well, thanks for your help, anyway."

He rang off.

"Not much help," he commented. "I thought we could have flushed them out by knowing their telephone number. Now, if they'd bought a farm, they would have the record changed, surely?"

"You'd think so."

"So I'm going to base my reasoning on the fact that they have the telephone installed; that they are on a farm, and that this farm does not belong to them. It is let to them for a short term. I suspect they paid a visit to Almond Grove this morning—something after nine. PC Jackson called, too, and there was some type of confrontation. They'd leave all together, and drive to their hideout. About eleven they rang Kennedy. An hour's drive away. Less, when you consider the problems of dealing with unwilling passengers, traffic and so forth. A farm, not more than thirty miles away from here; probably a damned sight less. Rented to them. How do we find it?"

"The estate agents . . ."

"Too many of them. Too time consuming—and besides, farms are let from great distances. You can find London estate agents who deal with farms in Yorkshire or even Scotland. No, we've got to find something local, something quick. Businessmen, tradesmen. . . ."

"But even in a small town like Southburn, there are scores of businessmen, all dealing with farmers. It would be a mammoth task. . . ."

"There must be some way," Purnell gritted his teeth. "There must be a way of finding out—someone will know if a farm has been vacant, or let. . . ."

"Scores of people will know, but it's a case of finding that one person who remembers one particular farm."

"The village policeman?"

"But we don't know which village, do we? The farm could be anywhere within a fifty miles radius of here. . . ."

"Insurance men!" cried Purnell. "They call on farmers."

"But there must be dozens of insurance

agents, some of whom pay visits to farms which are visited by other agents . . . Ah! . . . Got it!" Bailey snapped his fingers. "Got it!"

"Who?"

"The local NFU rep!"

"National Farmers' Union?"

"Yes. They deal with all sorts of problems appertaining to farms. Insurance, legal queries, a union for the workers. . . ."

"Who's the local chap?"

"Name of Waldron. Has a little office in town. Helpful chap."

"I'll ring him!"

Bailey looked up the number and dialled.

"No reply," he said. "He'll be out, calling on customers."

"Does he work special hours?"

"Nothing that can be called regular. I've often caught him at lunchtime when the telephone's switched through to his home."

"It's nearly lunchtime now."

"What will you do?"

"For lunch? I've asked Dickinson and Arden to call here and we'll find a café. Then I'd like a conference here. I'm expecting copies of the criminal records of Shaw and Bowry to arrive about two o'clock from NECRO. How far is it to Embleton?"

"Forty minutes by car. Thirty if you're rushing."

"Right. I'll see if they can rush one of their chaps over here—I'd like the one who dealt with the fatal accident that set this whole affair off. He must have something to offer us."

Purnell was quickly in touch with Embleton Police Office.

"Ah," he said when he won a response. "Crime Squad, Tees-side, Detective Sergeant Purnell speaking from Southburn. About that fatal of yours. Who dealt with it?"

Sergeant Tate said, "PC Christian."

"Any good?"

"First class policeman, if that's what you mean."

"What's he doing today?"

"Day shift—nine to five. He's gone home for lunch."

"What time's he due back?"

"One o'clock."

"Right. I'm having a panic conference here, in connection with the enquiry about that blue Jaguar. There's hell on here—got a missing policeman now. Could Christian come over please?"

"What time?"

"For two o'clock?"

"Sure. I'll ask the Superintendent, but he'll be allowed to come. Want him to bring anything?"

"His file on the accident, and details of that dead cyclist. Anything else that's of interest to us."

"I'll tell him."

"Good. Thanks a lot. We might get somewhere now."

As Purnell replaced the telephone, the office door opened and in walked Detective Constables Dickinson and Arden.

Arden looked very pleased with himself.

"You look like a dog with two tails," said Purnell, rising to his feet. "Learned something?"

14

"YES. I've got a smashing eye witness," said Arden, closing the door. "A woman—lives right opposite number twenty-eight," and he thereupon retold his story.

Dickinson settled himself in a chair and listened too; doubtless he'd been told the tale on his walk to the office, but for the two sergeants—Bailey and Purnell—this was interesting.

They let Arden finish in silence and he told a good story, keeping to the point and relating only the essentials.

"Great," beamed Purnell when he had finished. "So Jackson has been kidnapped. I don't think we can doubt that any more. But it's going to be one hell of a job finding him."

But as they chatted, Sergeant Bailey had picked up the list of stolen cars and was flicking through it carefully.

239

"What's that?" asked Purnell.

"Stolen cars. There was a Wolseley stolen locally, I'm sure. Within the last day or two. Somewhere on Teesside."

"Think it might be the one they're using now?" asked Purnell.

"More than likely. They've ditched that blue Jaguar after pinching it and using it under false plates. That accident put the wind up them; so they've nicked another one. It'll be under false plates too . . . ah!"

He stopped his examination of the list and said, "Here we are. Black Wolseley, 1954 model. Almost as new . . . belonged to a chap who's had it since new and barely used it. . . ."

"Is that one of the type used by the Yard at that time?"

"That's the one," said Bailey. "Right upset, he was. There was a paragraph in the Evening Gazette about it. He's kept it in peak condition all these years—only used it at weekends. A real gem, by all accounts, and then some swine goes and steals it! They've probably knocked hell out of it."

"There aren't many of them about now. It's a wonder it's not been spotted, especially after the papers have covered the item."

"Makes you wonder why they nicked it really—if it's our villains. You can understand a collector knocking off a beauty like that . . ."

"Maybe one of them is a collector, sergeant," put in Arden.

"Aye, that's more than likely," responded Purnell. "Right. Arden, old son. Get on that phone, will you? Ring our office in Middlesbrough and get an Express Message circulated to every policeman in the north of England. Tell them to look out for that stolen Wolseley with false plates. It's bound to carry them. Then look for PC Jackson—get a good description from Sergeant Bailey here. Also for Shaw, Bowry and Bourne-Atkins alias Shadwell. Mention in the message that there is a possibility that they'll be hiding on a recently-let farm.

You know the story. Give it the full treatment."

"Right."

"And in the meantime, gentlemen," said Purnell, "I'm going to find a nice café. Can't work on an empty stomach. Coming, anyone?"

"I'll come now," said Dickinson.

"I go home for mine," Bailey told them. "But stick the telephone through to me. I'll take any messages at home."

"We'll wait for Arden. Get a move on, lad."

"Ten minutes, Serge. You go ahead."

"Before you go to Southburn," said Superintendent Harris to PC. Christian, "I want a chat about that fatal accident."

"Yes, sir."

"Won't keep you long. Have we got the bike here?"

"It's down the cell passage, sir. Waiting there in case the coroner wants to look at it, or the court requires it as evidence."

"Good. I've been giving the matter a bit of thought, Christian. It really hinges on the lights, doesn't it? Simmons says there were none showing; the bike has lights fitted."

"That's true, sir."

"Have you examined the lights?"

"They were both smashed in the accident. Both bulbs are broken."

"But the batteries? I see from your enquiries at the pub where the bike was taken from that it was one which stays there, although no one claims ownership."

"Yes, sir. Left behind—anyone can use it."

"So no one will fit new batteries?"

"Only a person wanting to ride in the dark, I should imagine."

"Exactly, Christian. Exactly. So did the deceased fit new batteries before he rode away on it?"

"Well, I don't know . . ."

"But surely, Christian. It's a simple job to find out. Old batteries soon corrode, don't they? Have a look at them, will you?"

"Sir," and Joe Christian left the Superintendent's office.

It was one o'clock; the Super would be going for his lunch now, but there was time to pop down the passage before Joe left for Southburn.

He unlocked the heavy door which clanged open against the wall, switched on the dim lights and inspected the battered cycle. Already flakes of paint had been removed from it—they appeared to correspond with flakes removed from Simmons' car. Not that they would be necessary to prove the case in this instance, although they had been sent away for scientific analysis—just in case they were required. After all, Simmons could deny hitting the cyclist . . . he could. But no one would believe him—except maybe a doddering old Magistrate!

The lights. He tried to open the rear light, but it was stuck. With his penknife, however, he managed to prise out the reflector and saw the battery inside. Corroded. Green with heavy corrosion which had eaten into the interior of the rear lamp.

He was pleased for Simmons' sake.

Now the front one—just in case anyone suggested the bike might have been coming towards Simmons.

It was in a similar condition, corroded and messy, with never a hope of showing a light in that condition. Christian sighed. Why hadn't he done this before?

Then he heard footsteps; the Superintendent was striding towards him, cap and gloves on, leaving the office for his lunch at home.

"Well?" he asked, towering above the constable as he crouched before the cycle.

"Both corroded, sir."

"So they couldn't show lights?"

"Not a hope, sir."

"Mmm. That's in Simmons' favour. Decent chap, isn't he? Do you think it was careless driving, Christian?"

"I believed him when he said the cycle had no lights, sir."

"That doesn't answer my question, does it?"

"Not really. Well, sir, it's certainly not dangerous driving, is it? I mean, if the cycle had no lights. . . ."

"It is not dangerous driving, Christian. Therefore we cannot charge him with causing death by dangerous driving. That leaves a charge of careless driving to consider. Simple careless driving."

"Difficult, sir."

"I think it is careless driving, you know. Isn't it correct that a motorist should always drive so that he can pull up at any danger? This accident happened on a sharp corner—so Simmons should have eased off a little. Reduced speed. If it is a dangerous corner, and if it was dark and wet into the bargain, he should have been extra careful. Might have been cattle in the road; floods; pedestrians; a broken down car without lights. He never anticipated anything like that, did he? And, remember, he had been drinking."

"But we can't give evidence of that, sir."

"No, we can't. If we do, we must charge him with driving while impaired through drink or drug. No, I think there is a good case of driving without due care and attention. I'm going to authorize prosecution for that. See me about it when you return. You're going over to Southburn, eh? Got everything you require?"

"Yes, sir. Sergeant Tate's got everything out for me."

"Let me know what's going on over there. I've heard whispers of big time crime, but little else."

"Yes, sir."

As the Superintendent departed *en route* for his meal, Joe Christian locked up the cells, told the office duty man he was leaving, then took a police Ford Anglia out of No. 5 garage and started his journey.

He arrived in Southburn at ten minutes to two and parked in the neat yard at the side of the modern office. Then he entered.

"Ah!" said a man in plain clothes. "You must be PC Christian?"

"I am."

"Sergeant Purnell, Crime Squad. Nice you could come at such short notice. Find a chair and make yourself at home."

As Joe Christian settled down, Dickinson and Arden returned from their meal, and Sergeant Bailey returned from home.

"Photographs arrived yet?" asked Bailey.

"Not yet. I've rung my office—I'll get indigestion through rushing my meal to do it—and they're on their way here from Middlesbrough. Shouldn't be long."

"Right," said Bailey, "let's go through to the Muster Room, shall we? There's more space in there and we won't be interrupted by callers. I've got a man coming on duty at two—he'll look after the office and the phone."

The small contingent trooped through a sliding-door into an airy, spacious room lined with lockers. In the centre stood a large table with a green mock leather surface and it was surrounded by chairs.

"Help yourselves," invited Bailey. "How long will we be here?"

"Not long," said Purnell. "We can't afford the time. I want those bastards, and I want to find your lad, Jackson. But where do we look? That's one thing I want to iron out in this conference. That's why PC Christian's here—to see if there's any small link between his part of the world, and ours."

"I was thinking of a cup of tea at three o'clock."

"If we're here—yes. If not, no."

"Mmm," said Bailey. "We'll see. Have you tried that NFU man again?"

"No. I'll ring now before we start—we may as well wait until the photographs arrive."

Purnell dialled the number again; this time a woman answered.

"Police," announced Purnell. "I'm trying to locate Mr. Waldron, the Farmer's Union representative."

"I'm afraid he hasn't returned yet. This is Mrs. Waldron."

"Oh, dear. . . ."

"Can I ask him to ring you?"

"If he comes in before three. I'm

at Southburn Police Office—Detective Sergeant Purnell is my name."

"I'll ask him," she promised and rang off.

By now, a middle-aged constable was on duty in the office, and Purnell briefly told him about the conference.

Then a Volkswagen car turned into the yard and Purnell grinned, "My lads," he said. "Bang on time!"

He went out to meet two youthful detectives and chatted briefly to them; one of them passed him a large envelope, and then they came towards the office.

"You'd better come and sit in on our conference, lads," he was saying as he entered. "We might need your help."

Inside the conference room, he introduced the newcomers as Detective Constables Petty and Reed, from the Tees-side Crime Squad.

"Right," said Purnell, "we can start."

There was a murmur of approval, and a crashing of chairs as each man settled down at the table.

Purnell started the proceedings.

"Well, gentlemen, we are here to find four men. One is a policeman; three are crooks. We have reason to believe the policeman has been forcibly abducted by them, and we want to know where he is and what the men are up to in our area. But the whole affair started with a fatal accident. PC Christian—you dealt with it?"

"I did."

"Tell us about it? Take your time. Every detail is vital."

Joe Christian opened his file and began to relate the unfortunate experience of Henry Simmons. He told of the accident; the Jaguar at the farm entrance; the enquiries at the hotel and the two companions of the dead cyclist. He told of Henry Simmons' visitors . . .

When he had finished, Purnell began to ask questions.

"You said the cyclist's clothes were dry to a large extent. Yet it was a wet night —pouring down in fact?"

"Yes. I thought this indicated that he'd ridden only a few yards in the rain. From the barn, or from the Jaguar parked near the barn."

"Circumstantial evidence to connect him with the Jaguar. Now, this is important. The Jaguar was parked in a farm entrance?"

"Yes."

"There's a link I didn't realize until now. A farm. Who owns it?"

"I don't know. It's not my area, Sergeant. I went out to the accident because the local policeman was on leave."

"Can you find out? Ring the local PC. We must know who owns that particular farm. Ring when I've finished asking questions. Right. My next query is about the pub—the Grapes Inn, wasn't it?"

"Yes."

"The landlord, if I understand you correctly, saw two men with Cosford—or the man he thought was Cosford. We know he was, in fact, Edmunds, now dead."

"He told me so."

"Could he identify them?"

"I got the impression when I interviewed him that he didn't pay too much attention to these men. He said they were smartly dressed—typical of his clientele."

"It's of no consequence at this moment, but it might be important later. I must produce evidence that Shaw and Bowry were known to the dead cyclist. I'll have copies of their photographs run off for you."

"Thanks."

"Now, this insurance man. Simmons. Sensible sort of chap, is he?"

"I'd say so."

"Honest?"

"Oh, yes," said PC Christian with strong conviction in his voice. "Real nice chap."

"He identified that Jaguar when it went past his house?"

"Yes."

"Has he seen the drivers?" The question came quickly. Joe Christian said, "Yes, they. . . ."

Then his voice tailed off. He hadn't told the conference about Simmons' visitors and their threats to beat him and his family . . . that had been a man-to-man talk. . . .

"PC Christian," said Sergeant Purnell, "you're hesitating. Might I suggest they called on Mr. Simmons and uttered threats? That seems to be their usual practice."

Joe Christian knew he was talking to a seasoned, intelligent and highly successful detective Sergeant. He must tell the truth—this was an important crime enquiry, with a policeman's life at stake. . . .

"Yes, I should have mentioned it earlier. Simmons was visited by two men and, in fact, he was beaten. His wife and children have been threatened if he gives any further information to the police. He told me this, man-to-man. He's scared, dead scared."

"He has a right to be. Anyway, I'm not going to press the matter, except to say that I'd like you to show him the photographs of our two chief suspects. Ask him if he has seen them before—no need to say you've told us about the threats. That would destroy his confidence in you."

"I'll do that."

"Good. You realize that his positive identification would establish a much needed link between the cyclist and the suspects."

"I see that."

"Good. So you've three jobs. Find out about the farm near the scene of the accident, and show the pictures to two witnesses."

Purnell then turned to the rest of the gathering and said, "Anyone else want to ask PC Christian any questions?"

He was asked about one or two minor points, and his answers clearly satisfied all their queries. When he had finished, he went through to the Enquiry office to ring up about the farm.

"Right." Sergeant Purnell was in fine form today. "The next thing that happened was that a Mr. Charles Barnett, the boss of Henry Simmons, circulated a description of the blue Jaguar. He got the description from Simmons who wanted its driver as a defence witness. Barnett notified all his local agents. You heard what PC Christian said about Simmons' Star Man award—that is the motive behind Barnett's rather forceful public spiritedness. However, a blue Jaguar, answering the description of the one they sought, was seen outside twenty-eight Almond Grove, Southburn, the home of a man called Bourne-Atkins.

James Kennedy saw it, recognized it, and was ringing details to Barnett when he was stopped in the act. He was taken away and beaten up. PC Jackson now enters the story. He has not been found, by the way, but Sergeant Bailey is familiar with that side of the enquiry. Care to carry on, Sergeant?"

As the Sergeant spoke, PC Christian returned to his seat and listened intently.

He told of Jackson's keenness; his suspicions about Bourne-Atkins, his impetuosity; his talks with Kennedy; his visit to the hospital. . . .

When he had finished, Purnell again asked pointed questions.

"Thank you, Sergeant Bailey. You all heard that. For your information James Kennedy now has police protection. Now, Sergeant, I understand there was a bit of a hooh-hah about lack of action after Kennedy's phone call was cut short by our suspects?"

"There was, unfortunately. An understandable lapse."

"We all learn by mistakes. Now, Jackson seems to be a hell of a good policeman. He went to Middlesbrough General Hospital?"

"Yes."

"Because Kennedy was taken there by a motorist who found him staggering in a lonely lane?"

"Yes."

"And, according to what Jackson wrote in the Occurrence Book, Kennedy was beaten up in a barn—at a farm entrance, somewhere unknown?"

"Yes."

"Then that's it! That's the bloody place we're looking for!"

"Their hide-out?"

"Yes. A farm. Another bloody farm. Find that and we've got them!"

"But Kennedy can't remember where it was, Sergeant! He was battered into insensibility; they drove through that estate with him under duress in the back of the Jaguar. He hasn't a clue where he went—I'm sure he's not stalling there."

"I'm sure you're right. So where did he go? Can we find out?"

"I could ask him."

"No," said Purnell, who had spent some time with Jim Kennedy. "He didn't tell me. He couldn't tell me either. But. . . ."

Petty interrupted. "Who took him to hospital?"

Purnell cried with delight, "Got it! He was taken there by a passing motorist. The hospital should have his name. Petty—job for you. Find out who that motorist was; get round to see him now, or see his family. He must have talked about his adventure. All I want to know is which road he was on at the time. I want to

258

know where exactly he picked up the injured man, Kennedy."

Petty got up and left the room.

"If God is willing," said Purnell rather surprisingly, "we've got those swine."

In their hideout, George Shaw and Bill Bowry stood and looked down at the floor.

"There'll still be blood in the cracks, George."

"But it's not immediately obvious now, is it? We'll find a rug and lay it down there. I've been round with a duster, wiping off fingerprints where I think we've left them. I'll do this room immediately before we leave."

Bill nodded, "That's about it then? There's a lot of stuff in that far cowhouse. . . ."

"If I take the cattle truck loaded with the stuff, and you follow in the Wolseley?"

"Right. I'm famished, George. What time is it?"

"Quarter past two."

259

"Time for a snack. Load up the truck and then fire the barn?"

"Then away we go, never to be seen again!"

"I'll be glad to get out of here, I can tell you."

15

THE listening and questioning by Detective Sergeant Purnell continued in a speedy, but effective manner. Next on his list was Dickinson who had little to report, save for the condition of the interior of number twenty-eight Almond Grove and there were few questions.

Arden then said his piece, relating his conversation with Mrs. Campbell. She had proved a good witness; women usually were when they had time to observe, and her evidence would be invaluable.

When he had finished his account, Sergeant Bailey asked, "The time, Mr. Arden? Can we be sure she saw them just after nine?"

"Yes, I asked her about that. She was getting organized for a shopping trip and took particular note of the time."

Bailey continued, "Did you press her for further details of Bourne-Atkins?"

"I did ask her about him, but he was somewhat of a stranger to her. You know —big-house-on-the-corner type of person. Didn't mix with his neighbours by all accounts."

"So she didn't really know him?"

"Not personally—knew him by sight though."

"Thanks. Good job you went back to her house, Mr. Arden. Many wouldn't have bothered."

Arden smiled at the remark, and was pleased it had achieved results. There was a few moments silence, then Sergeant Purnell introduced Detective Constable Reed.

"I think," he said, "that each of us should be familiar with the events leading up to the current enquiry. We are not concerned here with the outcome of the possible charge against Henry Simmons, but we are interested in Messrs. Shaw and Bowry. What are they doing here? Where are they now? Why kidnap a police constable? These are the questions. Now, DC Reed. You have copies of their records?"

"I have, Sergeant."

"Read them out and pass their photographs around. We'll need copies running off eventually, if we are to prove anything against them and their cyclist. But that comes later. Off you go, then."

Reed started. He couldn't say much, but he did give details of the convictions against these two. Then he passed their photographs around.

"You perhaps know," he said, "that photographs of Bourne-Atkins, under his real name of Shadwell, are on their way, and all these men—apart from the cyclist —have one thing in common."

"Convictions for receiving stolen property?" put in Joe Christian, speaking his thoughts aloud.

"Yes. That may or may not be significant," added Purnell. "But it does give us two links now. Farms and stolen property. Is there a logical link between those two unlikely topics?"

"Storage space," put in Sergeant Bailey. "Large vehicles aren't uncommon in the vicinity of farms and any average farm has got dozens of outbuildings, many of them dry and warm even though they're not used. I'd say there's a very strong connection between the two."

"I respect your views," put in Purnell. "Anyone disagree?"

No one replied.

"Anyone any other ideas?"

Dickinson spoke, "I wonder if we're jumping into this with a little too much confidence in our own guesswork, because it is guesswork, you know. I'm wondering if we're overplaying the farm bit."

"Overplaying it?" asked Purnell.

"The blue Jaguar was waiting, or concealed in a farm entrance; Kennedy was beaten up in a dutch barn, again at a farm entrance, and Sergeant Purnell heard hens when he was rung from what might have been a farm. That's all we have to go on."

"All? I think it's a lot," Sergeant Bailey

spoke with a firm conviction in his voice. "It's a link. A link we can't ignore."

There was a knock on the door, and the office constable entered.

"Phone," he said. "For PC Christian."

"Excuse me," said Christian as he left the room.

He picked up the receiver and announced himself. "Embleton office here, Joe. Sergeant Tate. You've been ringing Demster about that farm?"

"I rang him direct."

"He didn't get the message too clearly —thought you were ringing from here. I said I'd relay the message though. Ready?"

"Go ahead, Serge. I hope he knew what I was after."

"This is what he said. The farm is called Hawthorn Hill Farm and is owned by an elderly man called Riley. In his seventies. Canny old character, and very well off by all accounts. He's got six other farms in this area."

"Has he?" cried Christian. "Do we know where they are?"

"Yes. Demster has a list—he checks all the stock records for these farms when he calls. Keeps a running total of visits for his monthly return."

"Can I have the farms?"

Sergeant Tate read them out and Christian jotted them down. All within an hour's reach of either Drydale or Teesside—they were situated in an area roughly between each locality.

When the list was complete, Christian asked, "Any idea what system he has for letting these?"

"He has a manager in them all. The profits are Riley's—he runs the farms in effect, and pays the managers a salary."

"He doesn't let them then?"

"No."

"Would PC Demster know if there was any change in managers?"

"No. He wouldn't necessarily be informed if a new manager was appointed, because, so far as Movements of Animals records are concerned, that doesn't matter. All the books are kept in the old man's name."

"Did he mention the blue Jaguar to Riley?"

"He hasn't seen Riley about this, Joe. Like I said, he got the details from his own records."

"Oh, of course. Anything else, Sergeant?"

"No. He didn't put forward anything else, Joe."

"Thanks. I'll give this list to Sergeant Purnell," and Joe Christian rang off.

He returned to the conference room to find them still discussing possible criminal activities, and he found that Petty had returned in the meantime. He must have used a phone on another extension.

"Ah, that's everyone back," said Purnell. "Right. Mr. Petty—let's hear your news?"

"I rang the hospital like you said, Sergeant. The man who took Kennedy in gave the name Thompson, Barlborough."

"That all?"

"I'm afraid so. He didn't stay long—he was a young man, going to meet his girl friend in Redcar, apparently. He left almost as soon as he had arrived at the hospital."

"Have you managed to find out where he lives?"

"Yes. 8 Main Street, Barlborough. It's a small village in the hills behind here."

"I know Barlborough," grunted Bailey. "In fact, I know Thompson, too. His dad is a wrong 'un."

"Can we interview him?"

"Young Thompson works on Tees-side —somewhere in ICI. We'll have a job finding him."

"How did you get his address then?" asked Purnell.

"Rang the post office in Southburn— the postmaster looked in the electoral registers for Barlborough."

"Good. OK. So he was picked up somewhere between Barlborough and Redcar. How far is that? How many farms on the route he would take?"

"It's six miles," said Bailey. "Upwards of a dozen farms on that road. . . ."

"Then he'll have to be interviewed. Is

there a security office or a police station within the ICI boundaries?"

PC Christian butted in. "Wait," he cried. "Barlborough. I might save time. I've got word about the farm entrance where the blue Jaguar was first seen. Hawthorn Hill Farm, just out of Drydale. Owned by an old chap called Riley. He's a wealthy farmer, and runs six other farms. I've got a list of them, and one is at Barlborough."

"Is it by Jove!" cried Purnell. "Whereabouts in Barlborough?"

"It's called Birch Hill Farm, Barlborough."

"Got an Ordnance Survey map?" asked Purnell of Bailey. "An up-to-date one?"

"In my office," and Bailey left to fetch it.

He returned and spread the map across the table and pointed out the town of Southburn.

"This is us. Now. Barlborough lies to the south, at the foot of the Cleveland Hills. Ten miles from here, I'd say."

"But in the Redcar direction?"

"Yes. There's a direct route from the village into Redcar—country lane, but direct nonetheless."

Bailey's finger traced the road, pausing at named farms, and then he cried, "Got it! Birch Hill Farm. A mile out of Barlborough, on the Redcar side. The farm stands nearly a mile off the road."

Purnell licked his lips, and said quietly, "A raid. We must raid it. Which other farms are owned by Riley?"

Joe Christian reeled them off. Beech Hall, Frythorpe; Oak Tree Lodge, Tilbury; Ash Farm, Carlton and Pine Forest Lodge, Carlton; Alder Park House, Alder Park, Manford.

"All trees, eh? All named after trees," commented Arden.

"So they are! I'll bet Riley's an eccentric old millionaire who buys up all farms with tree names. You get people like that, you know," chuckled Purnell. "Where are those in relation to Birch Hill?"

"Miles away," said Christian. "Three of them are near Embleton—the two Carlton ones and Manford."

Purnell gazed down at the map.

"Birch Hill Farm, Barlborough. Your Sergeant at Embleton said Riley's farms were run by managers, so there should be a manager in that one?"

"Yes."

"Not a couple of crooks . . ."

"Names? Did you get the names of the managers?" asked Dickinson.

"No, they're all under Riley's name," said Joe Christion; and then he said, "The telephone, Sergeant. Look in the telephone directory. Under Riley's name— ring them all, leaving Birch Hill till the end. Check on names in that manner."

"By George he's got it," chuckled Purnell. "I'll do it now."

He went through to the telephone armed with the list of farms, and checked the numbers in the directory.

"You're right," he told Christian. "Riley is shown at each of those addresses. OK. I'll try Manford first— Alder Park House."

He dialled the number and waited. The others were with him, expectant.

271

Petty said, "It's not many enquiries that can be dealt with via the telephone directory!"

But Purnell was speaking.

"Hello. Mr. Riley?" he asked, winking at the others. "No," said the voice. "This is his farm manager."

"Oh, it says in the directory . . ." began Sergeant Purnell.

"It's his farm," came the blunt reply. "My name is Sherwin. If you want Mr. Riley in person, you'll have to ring him at Drydale. Drydale 203."

"Thank you," and Purnell rang off.

"Sherwin's the manager of that one," he said and Arden jotted the name down.

Purnell continued through the list of farms, on each occasion pretending he was seeking Mr. Riley, and he reached the fourth one on the list—Oak Tree Lodge, Tilbury.

His enquiry was the same, but the result was slightly different.

"Riley's not here," came the reply. "We're all managers, you know. He's at Hawthorn Hill . . . always getting calls here, we are. Don't know why he doesn't let us use our own names."

"That would be the sensible thing when you're managing the place," put in Purnell, by way of sympathy towards the irate farm manager.

"Leastways," came the reply, "we were all managers. He's let off Birch Hill . . ."

"Birch Hill?" Purnell tried to sound puzzled.

"Bottom of the list in the telephone directory, near Barlborough."

'Oh," said Purnell. "Will that be changed then—to the tenant's name?"

"No idea. Queer characters . . . can't understand Mr. Riley . . ."

"Who's in that farm then?"

"No idea," came the response. "Not been there long. Queer chaps. Don't mix with us managers."

"Then Mr. Riley won't be there?"

"No. Try his Hawthorn Hill number; doesn't often go out."

"Thanks."

Purnell rang the fifth farm, Beech Hall, Frythorpe, and a woman answered and said her husband, John French, was in the fields. She advised the caller to ring Drydale 203 if he wanted Mr. Riley in person and Purnell thanked her.

"Well," he said, rubbing his ear after his lengthy conversation, "that's the first five eliminated. I've got all their names, and I haven't rung the Barlborough Farm."

"Any of them mention it?" asked Christian.

"Oak Tree Lodge. The manager there —I didn't get his name—said some queer characters were at Birch Hill Farm, Barlborough. Not been there long and didn't mix with the other managers. He felt they weren't managers—more like tenants."

"Are you going to ring that farm as well?" asked Sergeant Bailey. "The result will be a voice, won't it? And no one here has heard the suspects speak, have they?"

"I have," said Purnell. "One of them rang Kennedy while I was there."

And he gave a brief account of his talk with Jim Kennedy, then he was dialling the number of Birch Hill Farm, Barlborough.

At Birch Hill Farm the personal belongings of the two men, Shaw and Bowry were in the farm kitchen, in six suitcases.

George looked down at them. "You didn't leave any prints, anywhere?"

"No," replied Bill. "Not one. Wiped the lot."

"This is the house clear then. How long will it take to load the cattle truck?"

"Thick end of an hour, George. We've nearly forty TV sets for a start, then all those small electrical goods—transistors, steam irons . . ."

"Let's put these cases in the car, then, and get cracking. Can't leave the stuff behind, we'll need the money."

"I think we'd better blow," said Bill. "It's four hours or more since we vanished with that copper . . . they'll have missed him."

"If we panic, Bill, we've had it. Hurried departures always attract attention. We've got him and that silly old coot

Shadwell safely out of sight. What have we to worry about? So let's behave as if nothing has happened . . . we'll soon be on our way. The barn will be blazing like hell. There'll be no evidence to show that we were ever here."

"I don't like it. . . ."

"Aw, come on. Get packing."

Then the telephone rang.

"Who the hell's that?" snapped Bill, jerking round at the sound.

"Someone who knows us. Look—like I said. Act normal, Bill. Let me past— I'll answer it."

George picked up the receiver and said, "Birch Hill Farm."

A voice said, "Is that Mr. Riley?"

"No, it isn't, mister," replied George. "He doesn't live here. You want Hawthorn Hill Farm, Drydale. Can't think of the number offhand—I'm new here."

"I see," said the voice. "Thank you very much."

"Not at all, mister," grinned George and, as he answered, he bowed in mock subservience to the unknown caller. "Happy to oblige."

Bill grinned at George's small show of forced carefree abandon, and as George replaced the receiver, he said, "There. A simple call—someone looking for old Riley. Now, let's get the stuff packed."

Purnell put the telephone down and they looked at him, eager and expectant.

"Well?" asked one of them.

"The voice said, 'No, it isn't, mister' in reply to my first question, and later it said, 'Not at all, mister'."

"You recognized it then?" asked Arden.

"It was the man who rang Kennedy. I'd swear to that in a court of law," said Purnell.

"Do you think PC Jackson will be there, too?" asked Bailey.

"As one of us said earlier, there are plenty of warm, dry places on a farm where things can be hidden. Even people."

"Or bodies," said Arden, almost under

his breath. His remark drew one or two angry glares from the party, but Purnell was in charge again.

"Right," he said. "A raid on that farm. Come on lads. There's no time to lose. Let's work out a plan of action."

"Just us?" asked Bailey.

"And a couple of firearms, please," requested Detective Sergeant Purnell.

16

"THERE are three approaches to the farm," said Purnell. "Two from the road—one from either direction, that is. And the third is from the rear."

"The woods, you mean?"

"Yes. From the hills, through the woods."

Bailey frowned, What about waiting until night?

"Haven't time. Crooks move at night. I want to surprise them; and I want to reach them without them seeing us," Purnell told him. "And from those hills, we can look down upon them. Now, personal radios? Got any?"

"Three sets and a spare one. Issued to the station."

"All in working order?"

Sergeant Bailey nodded.

"Good. We'll need three parties to raid the place. . . ."

"Have we enough men here?" Sergeant Bailey sounded apprehensive. "We don't know how many are on that farm."

"I'd like more," Purnell agreed. "But that would take time. I didn't anticipate a siege or a raid. I set off this morning on a fairly routine enquiry, so, I think we'll make do. How many are we?"

"Eight," counted Bailey.

"Eight for three parties." Purnell was drawing a rough sketch of the area. "I'll need a uniform man with every party for a start."

Bailey said, "Right. Uniform men fall out into three corners. Me, Christian and the office man—PC Fairhurst."

They obeyed.

Purnell took over. "I agree. Sergeant Bailey, I'll put you in the first car. Arden and Petty, go with Sergeant Bailey. I'll suggest your duties in a moment."

Petty and Arden moved into the corner with Bailey and stood in silence.

"The second car," Purnell said, "will

also have a uniform man. PC Fairhurst—the office man. Can he be spared?"

"For this he can. If we have radios we'll be in contact with Divisional Headquarters."

"Good. PC Fairhurst, then. The second car with Detective Constable Reed."

"Two of us?"

"Yes. You'll see why in a moment. The remainder—myself, Dickinson and PC Christian will attack the farm from the hills."

Bailey signified his agreement.

"Now," Purnell was saying, "you only have two rifles?"

"That's all."

"And four radios?"

"Yes, but all the cars are radio equipped, remember."

"So is our car. Right, this is my plan. . . ."

By four-thirty that same afternoon, Purnell's men were in position. Purnell with his two colleagues, Dickinson and PC Christian had motored on a circular route and had parked their vehicle on the hills above the rear of the farm. The final mile had been too rough for the car, so they had walked, taking care to travel beneath the skyline.

Now, at four-thirty, they waited in the thick wood behind the farm, watching it and the country lane beyond. Dickinson had the rifle and a box of .22 ammunition; Sergeant Purnell had a radio and Christian had to rely on his uniform.

"Cattle truck in the farmyard," announced PC Christian.

"And two men loading it . . . bulky stuff by the look of it. Certainly not cattle!"

"Crickey! I hope Bailey isn't late. I said half-past four at the entrance to the farm."

"He's coming. From the left—from Redcar. See?"

PC Christian pointed and they could see the familiar shape of a black police Anglia moving swiftly towards the dutch barn at the farm entrance.

"Any sign of Fairhurst in the other car? He's coming in from the village."

"He's parked about half-a-mile up the lane," said PC Christian.

"Good. I'll call them up."

Sergeant Purnell pressed the switch on his personal radio and spoke.

"Green One to Green two and three over."

"Receiving—Green Two out."

"Receiving—Green Three out."

"Good. I'm going down through the woods now, towards the farm. Don't move until I give the word. For your information, a cattle truck is being loaded with boxes in the farmyard. Green Two —are you receiving?"

"Loud and clear," came the familiar voice of Sergeant Bailey.

"When I say 'Ready', will you move into the track leading to the farm. I'd say it was nearly a mile across the fields. Can you see it?"

"Yes—right to the house."

"Then drive up to the house, and block the lane with your car, just below the house. But for God's sake don't sit in the car! Surround the farm; keep under cover where possible. Remember you're not armed."

"I understand."

"After that, you're on your own. Right? Green Three—are you receiving?"

"Yes," came the heavy voice of PC Fairhurst, a constable of almost twenty uneventful years in the police service.

"Good. When you see Sergeant Bailey drive into the lane, you reverse in after him, but leave your car in the entrance, facing out into the lane—for a quick getaway if necessary. But you and Reed leave the car and get under cover in that dutch barn."

"I can see it."

"Take the rifle with you. Cover Sergeant Bailey and watch for anyone bolting across the fields. Don't be frightened to use that rifle if necessary. . . ."

"I'd be happier with a twelve-bore," grunted Fairhurst, who then added, "but they won't get past me, Serge."

"Right. I'm moving down through the woods now. The others are with me."

"The best of British," came Bailey's voice and then the radios fell into silence.

"That's the last box," said Bill. "All clear now."

"Right. Lock her up then. I'll get the car out, ready for off. It is loaded, isn't it?"

"The lot."

"Fine. The house is clear; the buildings are clear of loot. Just the barn, then?"

"That's all. Where do we meet afterwards?"

"The Highwayman, Highgate? To-morrow night—half-past seven?"

"Fair enough," agreed Bill. "You taking the car?"

"If you like—it's hot, but I don't think it will be spotted on the A1. Your truck OK?"

"All the documents are in order—it belongs to Riley. He's seen to everything."

"Right. Just the barn then? Got some petrol?"

Bill nodded. "I've got a five gallon drum ready. It's standing just inside at this very moment."

"Right. Let's start the engines. Want a hand to fire it?"

"No. You get in the car—go first. I'll follow in the truck and we'll part company immediately."

"We haven't told him anything, except that we're using his premises. Right?"

Seconds later, the engines of both vehicles were ticking over in the farmyard, and Bill said, "You go first, George."

"I want to see flames coming from that barn first! It contains a lot of bloody evidence!"

Bill didn't reply, but trudged across the vastness of the yard and disappeared into the dutch barn.

Inside, he halted and peered at what was soon to be the funeral pyre of two men. A young, ambitious policeman, now dead, and an aged crook who had come to a sticky end.

Loose hay was piled deep and thick over the corpses, and the walls of the barn were lined with similar bales. When this was soaked with petrol, it would go up in a flash . . .

Bill lifted the can; the petrol sloshed about inside as he carried it towards the area which concealed the bodies. He could feel the wind now. Cold and easterly, blowing through the barn. That was a godsend.

He took off the top of the petrol can and threw it behind him; it clanged on to the earthy floor and rolled away, coming to rest near the door. Now he was throwing petrol all about him; soaking the hay, filling the air with its pungent fumes. Five gallons was a lot when it only came out in drops.

He began to pour it, holding the handle in his left hand, and the base in his right, teeming pint after pint upon the hay.

He was sweating; the thought of his actions, the frenzied activity of these moments. He stood a moment to regain his breath, the can dangling empty from his fist.

He threw it aside; it fell with a hollow sound to the floor, and he produced a box of matches from his trousers pocket.

He knew the ferocity of petrol-soaked hay; he stood back from his ignition area, took out a match and struck it.

It flared into a tiny orange flame; he waited until the match was well alight and then tossed it.

The light faded away and it fell dead into the hay.

"Damn!"

Another one; he struck the second match and waited a little longer. It was burning well; he tossed it.

It fell on to the waiting pile. It lay for the briefest of moments, and then there was a whoosh; a hollow sound and a mass of flame spread across the petrol and the hay, sending a quick blast of heat at the man responsible, and throwing a pall of heavy grey smoke into the free air of the barn.

Bill ran.

"Go," he shouted at George in the Wolseley. "Go. She's going like hell!"

And flames were already leaping from the barn.

Purnell saw them lock the cattle truck, and he saw George settle into the driving seat of the Wolseley.

"Green One to Green Two and Three. They are about to move off. Are you in position?"

Bailey's answer came first, "Arden and Petty are circling the farmhouse now. No sign of activity at this side. I'm with the car—it's across the track near the end of the house. They can't get through."

"Good. And Green Three?"

Fairhurst's voice came back. "Like you said, Serge. Car waiting for the off. Reed's in the dutch barn, waiting for 'em to bolt. I'll stay near the car for the time being."

"Good. Now, one of them is sitting in the Wolseley; the other's going into a dutch barn. The big one with the green roof. Probably going for a run off . . ."

"Any sign of Jackson?" asked Bailey suddenly.

"No. Just two of them; Shaw and Bowry, I'd say."

"Wonder where the hell Jackson's gone?" and Bailey's radio went dead.

"The Wolseley is waiting for the other chap . . . get ready for them bolting. We must get them with the evidence. . . . God Almighty!"

"What?" screeched Bailey.

"Fire! They've set fire to that bloody barn. Going like hell, it is. . . ."

"I'll radio for the Brigade . . ." shouted Bailey. "Jackson . . . in that barn! Jackson will be there. . . . The bastards. . . ."

His voice trailed off.

Purnell ran. Dickinson and Christian ran.

But the Wolseley was already rolling away.

And the driver of the cattle truck was in his seat.

17

"**S**TOP!" cried Purnell leaping over the wall into the farmyard. "Stop! Police!"

He saw George's look of sheer amazement . . . the Wolseley leapt away; PC Christian also leapt over the wall, rapidly followed by Dickinson.

"Cops!" hissed George to himself. "They're onto us . . . come on . . ."

He urged the car to top speed, swung left past the end of the house and cried out in anger and disappointment. A black Anglia blocked the farm road.

He flung himself across the wheel, the car careered across the unmade track, tyres tearing at the rough surface, and it collided with the rear of the Ford.

George was out.

Running for the house; the policeman was running towards him, shouting "Stop!"

But he was at the door. He was in. He slammed the door and rammed home the massive bolt, panting with fear and abject terror.

Cops! Watching them . . . here all the time . . . watching and waiting. . . .

Upstairs. Shot-gun on the wall . . . in the kitchen. Always there. . . .

He looked wildly about him, saw the double-barrel gun slung along a beam of the kitchen, and seized it with both hands. Cartridges in the drawers.

That top drawer in the old chest.

Box of them, almost full.

Panting and almost crying with fright, George stuffed his pockets full of cartridges; behind him there was a hammering on the door. Smoke. From the barn. Thick and heavy.

Bill?

Outside there was a roaring of the giant engine from the cattle truck.

But George must get upstairs. Could he escape? There was a back staircase to this house . . . all the old farms had two staircases. One for the family, and one for the workers who lived in. The servants' quarters . . .

And a back door.

There was another back door. It led outside, through the machine house, out behind the buildings, into that ploughed field or the woods. The woods. He'd be safe there . . .

He ran for the staircase.

And all the time the engine of the cattle truck revved and roared; at its wheel sat Bill and the vehicle was rolling past the side of the house.

Coppers. Running. Shouting. George panicking as usual.

Bill let out the clutch and the heavy truck responded; it entered the track alongside the house.

"The silly bastard!"

It was blocked with the Wolseley and a Ford. A police Ford. Police? He could see only those behind him. He hadn't heard that Ford. . . .

He accelerated. The massive weight of the wagon rammed into the rear of the

Wolseley; it was pushed partly through the hedge on Bill's right.

He slammed his vehicle into reverse; then forward again. He rammed it into the Wolseley and the Ford.

Again.

And again.

The Wolseley now gave him room to pull through; the Ford was still in the way. But it had shifted.

Then a Police Sergeant, running along the front of the house towards him, shouting.

Running towards the truck. Bill grinned . . . the bloody fool! Flesh and blood against a vehicle like this.

He rammed the Ford again. It bounced around. Another push and he'd be through.

The Sergeant, in uniform, was near him. He mounted the running board at the far side of his truck. Climbed up, hanging on to the door handle. Trying to open it.

Bill felt in his pocket. His pistol. The one he always carried. . . .

He was in reverse. He let out the clutch.

The truck bucked backwards; Bailey still clung on to the door.

"Down, or I'll shoot!" and Bill waved the pistol.

The Sergeant's face disappeared.

Forward again. Crashed through this time. With a rending of metal against metal and a harsh clanging, the cattle truck was through.

Bill heard the fading shouts of the Sergeant. They'd got poor old George. He'd never get out of there . . . God! The smoke. Hanging low now, and. . . .

Another bloody police car! In the entrance. A huge uniformed copper standing beside it.

Bill accelerated down the long lane; the cattle truck bounced and rocked across the rough track and it gathered speed as it made for the exit on to the road.

Would it withstand the next crash?

A little Ford . . . nothing to prevent it moving, apart from a handbrake.

Then Bill gasped.

Crouched a few yards from the car was the same huge policeman—he'd moved like lightning. Crouched there, his right knee in the furrows of the ploughed field, and in his hands a rifle, aimed directly at the truck.

And the policeman wasn't flinching. His aim was sure and steady, directly at Bill.

Bill eased off. . . .

What could he do? Surrender? Ditch the truck and run? Or carry on? Would that copper fire?

The English police were known for their reluctance to arm themselves, except in an emergency.

A choice. An unpleasant choice.

Bill Bowry chose to fight it out. He chose to ram the Anglia in the gateway; he chose to risk his life against the well published attitude of the English police.

But he had chosen the wrong man. He had chosen a policeman who had seen active service on the front line in France; he had chosen a fearless policeman as his adversary. He had chosen PC Alan Fairhurst.

He accelerated, heading for the Ford only yards away. The policeman raised a hand. The stop signal.

"Bugger off, copper," and Bill laughed. Derision, anger, frustration—all were contained in that laugh. A fake laugh of artificial bravado.

But the laugh died as a bullet crashed into the nearside front tyre. The lorry lurched violently, it careered to its left and the front wheel sank into the soft earth of the ploughed field.

But still it moved.

Bill cried, "Go on . . . go on. . . ."

But the lorry lurched to a grinding halt, as the policeman stood up, grinning.

Bill would stop that grin! He would wipe if off the face of that fat, trigger-happy copper. . . .

His pistol was in his hand. He waited in the cab; the lorry was tilted at an alarming angle, its offside wheels still on the hard surface.

A plain clothes policeman appeared as well. From the barn. Two of them. How many more?

"Get out!" bawled the uniformed policeman. "Get out of that truck, mate!"

Bill made as if to move; he opened the door carefully, the pistol tight in his grip.

Once that copper came level with him. . . .

Alan Fairhurst was no fool. He noted the sly movements of the driver, and he advanced carefully, gingerly.

The cab door was opening. The man leapt to the ground; then a pistol. Pumping shots. . . .

Fairhurst reacted swiftly; the years were swept away. He was back on the front line, back in France, back in the face of the enemy, young and alert. Hearing the whine of shells, the drone of aircraft, the smell of blood. Of fear. Fairhurst fell flat on his face; he fell deliberately into one of those furrows, and the rifle was pumping shots at the man, pumping fast and furious, alarming and accurate.

"Don't!" shouted the detective, running.

"Don't," screamed the falling lorry driver. "Don't . . . don't. . . ."

But the deed was done.

Lance Corporal Fairhurst had killed another of the menacing enemy.

George Edwin Shaw was on the top floor, nursing the shot-gun as he sought refuge. He'd heard them rattling the door down below, shouting at him, pleading with him to come out.

But he'd ignored them; he'd pretended not to hear them; he was alone in the vast emptiness of this house, barely furnished and poorly decorated.

Nothing.

He paused in a corridor to listen. Shouting outside; the crackle of flames from the barn, sparks blowing high and far in the easterly wind which swept across the plateau at the foot of those hills. Sparks blowing bright and clear against a leaden sky. He looked down into the yard.

One man in plain clothes in the centre, looking up at the upper windows; the barn ablaze and hot. Bill?

The cars would have stopped him. Poor sod. But he had the pistol; and he would use it.

God! That barn was like an inferno. . . .

George Edwin Shaw moved into the depths of the house, listening as he trod lightly on the carpetless floors. Apart from the crackle of flames, there was nothing.

No shouting. No footsteps. No banging on the doors. Nothing.

Where were they? How many of them?

A room; small with a dirty window. He hurried across the wooden floor and peered out. The cattle truck motionless near the gate, tilted at a crazy angle. Two men standing there and a Sergeant running.

They'd got Bill!

The big copper had a rifle. . . .

That's how they'd got Bill!

But they wouldn't get George Edwin Shaw. Back from the window, through to the servants' end of the house; through low-ceilinged rooms and on to a wide landing.

The second staircase, leading outside through the buildings. Through the granary, warm and dry; the saddle rooms, the stables at the far end, all unused for years.

He ran down the wooden staircase, clattering as he moved; there was a brown painted door at the bottom. It opened at his touch and he stepped into the room below. Stone-flagged floor, small and compact, with a black Yorkshire range . . . funny the things you noticed when you were in a rush. . . .

The outer door lay across the room from him. Into the buildings—and beyond that was the wood. The dense wood. Safety. Freedom.

He opened that door too. Confidently. He stepped into the deserted place.

A voice said, "George Edwin Shaw,"

and George gasped with surprise, with fright; then he recovered. He whirled around, shot-gun at the ready, but the young plain-clothes man had a grasp of its barrel. Pushing it upwards, forcing it away, pointing its twin muzzles at the high ceiling. . . .

George was sweating. . . .

"You are under arrest," said Detective Constable Arden. "This thing isn't a ha'porth of use now. . . ."

"Bastards . . . all of you . . . bastards" . . . and he flung the weapon away from himself; the impetus startled the detective who staggered backwards under the sudden release of pressure. He still grasped the weapon; it crashed against the door-post behind him, but there was no explosion.

But George was away. Running through the maze of outbuildings, seeking a door to freedom . . .

First door. Locked!

"Bastards! Bastards!" he shouted.

He ran, mad, frightened; like a captive hare he twisted and turned, and then the policeman was running after him, carrying the shot-gun.

But he wouldn't use it.

Then George was outside.

In the yard again; to his right the fire, fierce and hot, blazing furiously, throwing out smoke and heat and sparks. . . .

Another voice. "Only one exit, isn't there?" and the large hand of Detective Sergeant Purnell fell on his shoulder.

George Edwin Shaw wanted to be sick —two bodies lay in the yard, their clothes blackened and charred, the flesh scorched and burned, smoke still rising from them. They'd been dragged clear of the flames. . . . Clear!

"We found the petrol can," said the Detective. "You'll deny it, I know. But there are some excellent fingerprints on it . . . I'm sure our experts will be delighted to examine it."

And he took George away.

As they walked, a fire engine was negotiating the wreckage of the vehicles.

It would be needed to save the

farm; already the barn was a mere shell, but an outbuilding crackled into sudden fire.

"Come on," said Purnell. "It's too late now."

18

TWO days later on the Friday, the telephone rang at Hive Cottage, Drydale, and Henry Simmons answered it. It was early yet—barely nine-thirty, and he was skimming through his morning's correspondence.

"Embleton Police," came the familiar voice of PC Christian.

"Ah!" Henry cried. "I was hoping you'd ring—I read about that carry-on over at Barlborough. Were those characters my friends in the blue Jaguar?"

"That's the couple," said Christian. "Real swine, they were. Killed PC Jackson because he'd tumbled to their game, I think, and they killed Bourne-Atkins, alias Shadwell for some other reason. We're not certain yet why, but it looks like internal bother."

"What were they involved in?"

"All sorts of rackets, tied up together.

305

Receiving stolen goods, blackmail, protection rackets, mainly. That blue Jaguar of yours certainly set things off, Mr. Simmons."

"It was them, I gather?"

"Oh, yes. That farm where you first saw it belongs to old Riley."

"Nice old stick."

"Our CID have seen him, and it seems they'd approached him about a vacant farm and terrified him into letting it to them for next to nothing. That cyclist was a mate of theirs who had been brought here to supervise things for them. They'd taken him to the farm that night, and introduced him to old Riley; the idea was for them to go away for pastures new, while the cyclist—Edmunds—would take charge of their interests up here."

"And they terrified Riley into silence? Like they did with me and Kennedy?"

"That's it. They've been operating over a wide area, by all accounts, and have been offering 'protection' to certain premises and people in return for cash. Again, they used the terror system."

"What about the Bourne-Atkins fellow? Was he with them, too?"

"A long time ago, when he was in business, he helped to dispose of stolen property. He did this as a service for a lot of people and among his customers in this respect, were our friends Shaw and Bowry. Bourne-Atkins, or Shadwell as he should be known, got caught and disgraced, so he moved house. His wife died about the same time and he settled, under a new name, in Southburn. He changed his tactics and became totally law-abiding."

"But they found him?"

"They did. George Shaw told us about him. They decided they could use his services once more. He was therefore coerced into helping them, much against his will. The reason he denied seeing the Jaguar outside his house was because he didn't want his masters to think he'd been a police informer. So he denied everything—but when PC Jackson arrived at his house, they no longer believed him."

"So they killed him and PC Jackson?"

"Yes. And those men paid a visit to you . . . they're vile and ruthless. . . ."

"Oh God!" said Henry. "Thank God they won't return."

"Yes. You're safe enough now. The death of young Jackson and Shadwell started the panic. We recovered thousands of pounds worth of stolen property from their farm—they were using its commodious buildings as storage units. Periodically, they took a loaded cattle-truck down to London to sell their ill-gotten wares. Stolen on Tees-side and in the Durham area, and sold down south. As soon as this link was established, Edmunds—the cyclist—would have taken over. Shaw and Bowry would have moved elsewhere and done the same thing again."

"The swine! And they'd kill for greed!"

"More through panic, I'd say. Anyway, that case is closed, save for the inquest on Bill Bowry."

"Talking of inquests—heard any more about my case?"

"That's why I was ringing, actually.

The coroner hasn't definitely fixed the date yet, but before the inquest is opened, he wants to know the official outcome of your case."

"What's that? I assume you're ringing to tell me?"

"I am. Our Superintendent has read the report—and he's considered all the evidence, but regretfully, he has still decided to take you to court!"

"Oh, God!"

"On the least possible charge—careless driving. He alleges your carelessness was the result of not driving within your own stopping distance."

"Is that a serious charge?"

"Far from it. Some police forces summons every motorist who's involved in an accident. They invariably charge careless driving. The logic is that there must be some degree of carelessness in every accident, however slight that carelessness may be. However, it doesn't involve compulsory disqualification of your licence, and I know our magistrates will deliver fair judgment."

"Thanks for telling me. I suppose I was careless, really. . . ."

Margaret came in, and took his arm as he spoke. He listened to PC Christian giving him some indication of what to expect, then leaned across to kiss her.

She whispered to him. "Mr. Barnett's come. He's in your office."

Henry rang off after thanking PC Christian for his help.

"What's old Charlie want?" grunted Henry.

"About the Star Man award," she said. "He wanted to make sure you were still trying for it?"

"There's no peace, is there?" grumbled Henry Simmons.

Other titles in the
Linford Mystery Library:

A GENTEEL LITTLE MURDER
by Philip Daniels

Gilbert had a long-cherished plan to murder his wife. When the polished Edward entered the scene Gilbert's attitude was suddenly changed.

DEATH AT THE WEDDING
by Madelaine Duke

Dr. Norah North's search for a killer takes her from a wedding to a private hospital. She deals with the nastiest kind of criminal—the blackmailer and rapist!

MURDER FIRST CLASS
by Ron Ellis

A new type of criminal announces his intention of personally restoring the death penalty in England. Will Detective Chief Inspector Glass find the Post Office robbers before the Executioner gets to them?

CASE WITH THREE HUSBANDS
by Margaret Erskine

Was it a ghost of one of Rose Bonner's late husbands that gave her old Aunt Agatha such a terrible shock and then murdered her in her bed? The Bonner family felt that only Inspector Septimus Finch could catch the killer.

THE END OF THE RUNNING
by Alan Evans

Lang continued to push the men and children on and on. Behind them were the men who were hunting them down, waiting for the first signs of exhaustion before they pounced.

CARNABY AND THE HIJACKERS
by Peter N. Walker

When Commander Pigeon assigns Detective Sergeant Carnaby-King to prevent a raid on a bullion-carrying passenger train, he knows that there are traitors in high positions within the railway, banking and even police circles.

TREAD WARILY AT MIDNIGHT
by Margaret Carr

If Joanna Morse hadn't been so hasty she wouldn't have been involved in the accident, and wouldn't have offered hospitality to the injured woman, only to find she was an escaped inmate from the local nursing home.

TOO BEAUTIFUL TO DIE
by Martin Carroll

There was a grave in the churchyard to prove Elizabeth Weston was dead. Alive, she presented a problem. Dead, she could be forgotten. Then, in the eighth year of her death she came back. She was beautiful, but she had to die.

IN COLD PURSUIT
by Ursula Curtiss

In Mexico, Mary and her cousin Jenny each encounter strange men, but neither of them realises that one of these men is obsessed with revenge and murder. But which one?

LITTLE DROPS OF BLOOD
by Bill Knox

It might have been just another unfortunate road accident but a few little drops of blood pointed to murder—and plunged Chief Inspector Colin Thane and Inspector Phil Moss into another adventure.

GOSSIP TO THE GRAVE
by Jonathan Burke

Jenny Clark invented Simon Sherborne because her daily gossip column was getting dull. But when the society editor demanded a picture of the elusive playboy, Jenny knew she had to get rid of him. Then Simon appeared at a party—in the flesh! And Jenny finds herself involved in murder.

HARRIET FAREWELL
by Margaret Erskine

Wealthy Theodore Buckler had planned a magnificent Guy Fawkes Day celebration. He hadn't planned on murder.

36/6

0190